W. S. Walker

Between the Tides

Comprising Sketches, Tales and Poems, Including Hungry Land

W. S. Walker

Between the Tides
Comprising Sketches, Tales and Poems, Including Hungry Land

ISBN/EAN: 9783337090319

Printed in Europe, USA, Canada, Australia, Japan

Cover: Foto ©Andreas Hilbeck / pixelio.de

More available books at **www.hansebooks.com**

BETWEEN THE TIDES

COMPRISING

SKETCHES, TALES AND POEMS,

INCLUDING

H-U-N-G-R-Y L-A-N-D.

W. S. WALKER.

NO PLACE LIKE HOME.

LOS GATOS, CALIFORNIA

W. S. AND GLENN WALKER, Printers.

1885.

To MY FAMILY, who have been my companions in travel, who have shared my joys and sorrows, this Book is respectfully dedicated by

THE AUTHOR.

BETWEEN THE TIDES.

TABLE OF DISTANCES FROM SAN FRANCISCO
TO SOME OF THE PRINCIPAL POINTS IN CALIFORNIA.

For the following valuable table of reference, we are indebted to
H. S. CROCKER & Co., of San Francisco, Publishers of the RAIL-
ROAD GAZETTEER, and it can be relied upon as correct.

ALAMEDA, Alameda county.......................11 miles.
AMADOR CITY, Amador county................154 miles.
AUBURN, Placer county........................126 miles.
BIG TREES, Calaveras county...................169 miles.
BIG TREES, Santa Cruz county..................75 miles.
BIG TREES, Mariposa county...................250 miles.
CAMP CAPITOLA, Santa Cruz county............85 miles.
CLOVERDALE, Sonoma county.................84½ miles.
DONNER LAKE, Nevada county.................197 miles.
EUREKA, Humboldt county.....................216 miles.
GEYSER SPRINGS, Sonoma county.............100 miles.
HEALDSBURG, Sonoma county................66½ miles.
HOTEL DE REDWOOD, Santa Cruz county........66 miles.
HOTEL DEL MONTE, Monterey county..........125 miles.
HUMBOLDT BAY, Humboldt county.............216 miles.
LOS ANGELES, Los Angeles county............482 miles.
LAKEPORT, Lake county.......................119 miles.
MARTINEZ, Contra Costa county................36 miles.
MARYSVILLE, Yuba county....................142 miles.
MONTEREY, Monterey county.................125 miles.
NAPA, Napa county............................46 miles.
OAKLAND, Alameda county......................6 miles.
PETALUMA, Sonoma county.....................36 miles.
PLACERVILLE, Eldorado county...............148 miles.
RED BLUFF, Tehama county...................200 miles.
SACRAMENTO, Sacramento county..............90 miles.
SAN DIEGO, San Diego county................661 miles.
SAN JOSE, Santa Clara county.................47 miles.
SANTA BARBARA, Santa Barbara county........288 miles.
SANTA CRUZ, Santa Cruz county...............81 miles.
SANTA ROSA, Sonoma county...................52 miles.
STOCKTON, San Joaquin county................93 miles.
TAHOE CITY (Lake Tahoe), Placer county......224 miles.
YOSEMITE, Mariposa county..................285 miles.

CONTENTS.

BETWEEN THE TIDES.

INTRODUCTORY.

In presenting this work to the public, I do not promise, nor do I expect to produce anything of an unusually brilliant nature, and will endeavor to confine myself to language with which I am most familiar—plain household words; and if my efforts are crowned with any good results, it will be gratifying to the author. In short, if I cause a moment of serious reflection to the general reader, or create a good hearty laugh (even though it be at my misfortune), or persuade people (no matter where they live) to court contentment and let well enough alone—then, kind reader, let me say that I have not lived entirely in vain. And also, if I can succeed in disposing of this entire edition for about one hundred per cent above its actual cost, and two hundred per cent above its actual worth, leaving the undersigned just about three hundred per cent net profit, then my mission as a Book 'writist' will be accomplished.

In 1880, while at Cloverdale, Cal, I published a small pamphlet, entitled "Glimpses of Hungry Land," and as the little book met with considerable favor from the public; and upon the urgent solicitation of many friends, and also owing to having the little work copyrighted, I have concluded to include it in this my latest venture, and therefore offer the following explanation:

Hungry-land may be considered a peculiar and homely word when used in connection with the title of a book—perhaps it is; yet in this instance, Hungry-land figures as the home of the roving, discontented, dissatisfied and restless class of individuals to be found in every portion of the civilized world. Those individuals who are never contented, but alway restless, continually 'pulling up stakes' and moving around in search of something better, are always hungry. Their bodies, hearts, minds and pockets are hungry—in a word, they spend their lives in what to them is a hungry land; and as I belong to that unfortunate class, I can truly say that I write from experience; for I have been one of the many individuals who are loth to remain long enough in any one place to properly enjoy the blessings of this world.

This life is largely made up of Memory and Hope—both are dreams.

To a great extent we are creatures of circumstances, and as liable to change as the ever varying climate of our country. While standing, as it were, knee-deep amid the clover-fields of the present, how often we look forward to the gilded visions of the future, and quicken our steps and often go beyond our depth in the hurried effort to grasp the prize.

Then again, in fancy, how often we retrace our steps and bask in the sunny haunts of our youth and sigh for the return of those halcyon days; or perhaps we go still farther back, groping our way over the beaten track of ages, and mourn that we lived not in earlier times, mid scenes that have long been festooned with the dust of dead centuries. Truly, how few of us really live in the only period we can call our own—the PRESENT!

Imagination lends a charm to distance, and far-off objects often lose their brightness upon a near approach. We talk of days gone by when we were *so happy and contented*, when in reality were we to consult our old journals of every day life, we would discover the fact that we were just as miserable then as now. In those bewitching hours of the past that we so love to refer to, we were doubtless looking back or forward just the same as we are to-day. I claim as a general rule, that people blessed with the light of civilization enjoy very little true happiness on this earth.

We see individuals every day, who, to all exter-
nal appearances should be happy—people who
live in ease and luxury, at whose door WANT, that
cruel master never knocks; along whose pathway
the cares and shadows of the world seldom or
never come; yet even they go around with long
faces, bemoaning their fate, murmuring, fret-
ting, and declaring that everything is going
wrong. Verily, "such is Life."

There was a time, yet fresh in my m e m o r y
when the Far West looked to me most beautiful
as I stood on the fertile prairies of Illinois, surrounded with everything to render me happy—
at home, in a State, of whose vast resources a
World might well be proud; yet I grew discontented, and consequently unhappy. Of course I
was miserable. Everything seemed too common-
place. Life was monotonous. The old home circle lost its charms. From the friendly v o i c e s,
whose genial influence had surrounded me from
the sunny days of childhood to manhood's years,
I turned away with impatient feelings. The climate of old Illinois seemed too close and oppressive for me. I wanted fresh air; and I thought I
could find it "out West."

In the distance, with imagination's big teles-
cope to aid me, I beheld the Golden Land, clothed in robes of matchless beauty; her hills covered with verdure—the whole land be-decked with

flowers of gorgeous hue; with gold-lined ravines and silver-spangled ledges, whose ocean-washed and shell-strewn shore glistened and sparkled in the mellow sun-light of perpetual summer. Every vale seemed an elysian; every mountain, dell, nook and valley, the abode of true, romantic and unalloyed happiness.

Thus I gazed upon the Far West—the f a i r y isle of my imagination.　　　　　　W. S. W.

HUNGRY LAND.

By the Rivers and the Oceans,
  By the Mountains and the Lakes;
Mid the regions of the North-land,
  And the tangled Southern "brakes;"
From America's fertile borders,
  To her central belts of sand—
I have sought "a better country,"
  But found instead—the Hungry Land.

On the broad high-ways of travel,
  In the workshops, fields and mines;
In the cities, towns and hamlets,
  Where the sun of freedom shines:
I have found a band of brothers,—
  A discontented, roving band;
They are "men without a country,"
  For they live in Hungry Land.

They who pass their time in seeking
  For a road without a hill,
Have within their souls an empty space,
  This world can never fill;
For, no matter where we go,
  We find them hand in hand:—
The discontented and the roving—
  Dwellers in the Hungry Land.

For, no matter where your home is:
　On the land or on the sea;
A toiler in a monarch's realm,
　Or with the noble free—
Whether in a peasant's cottage,
　Or with wealth at your command,
If contentment dwells not in you,
　You live in Hungry Land.

But there is a "Better Country,
　In a clime beyond the Sun,
Where earth's trampers may find shelter
　When the toils of life are done;
Where their feet will never weary,
　As they tread the golden sand:
It's the country "over yonder,"
　Beyond the Hungry Land.

FROM ILLINOIS TO NEW YORK.

My mind was made up. I had fully determined to "go West." My valise was packed; and the time for my departure drew near.

On the morning of April 7th, 1864, a crowd of cherished relatives and kind friends assembled at my old home in Mason City, Illinois, bid me "Good-by and Farewell," and a few moments later I was "off for California." Since that time, more than twenty years have passed away, but the recollections of that soft Spring morning, the last good-by and hand-shake with loved friends, many of whom have long since been laid away beneath the sod— the long lingering look, as through blinding tears, I caught the last glimpse of my old home and the loved group, ere all faded from my sight, and—the great wide world was before me—still linger fresh in my memory.

The first day I went as far as Peoria, distant 40 miles, which for lack of railroad, I made the journey on a neighbor's wagon.

At Peoria I purchased a ticket for New York. I wished to go over the Michigan Central Railroad via. Suspension Bridge, and in asking for a ticket I committed an innocent blunder by calling for one to New York via. *Extension* Bridge!

The agent, fortunately happened to be out of the extended kind, but promptly furnished me with the proper pasteboard. The next morning I arrived in Chicago, but the train stopped here only long enough to admit of a hurried breakfast, and we were off again; and all that day, as we hurried along, I sat at a car window, gazing at the fertile fields, bustling towns and grand old forests that form the characteristic features of Michigan, until the shades of evening found us at the beautiful city of Detroit. Here we went on board a splendid ferry-boat, and were invited to 'sit right down to supper.' We were told by a pompous individual that it would be "policy to sit right down," as we would "have to pay coin for hash over in Canada." The majority of the passengers (including the author) paid our little fifty cent green-back and then we "sat right down," and just about the time we got ready to call for coffee the boat reached the Canada shore and an old sinner yelled in fiendish tones: "All aboard for Niagara." Of course we scrambled off the boat and hurried to the train, leaving the little supper farce on the boat to be played over again on the next load of passengers; and judge of our surprise when at the next station the gong sounded and as fine a looking man as I ever set eyes on sang out: "Twenty minutes for supper— and Greenbacks taken at par." In order to satisfy the cravings of my "Department of the Interior," I squandered another fifty-cent piece. All that night we rolled through Canada, but owing to the darkness and the lacerated state of my feelings over the Detroit ferry-boat supper, I was unable to form an intelligent opinion of the country,—however. "You can see it on the map."

While stopping for a few minutes at a station (just before daylight), we caught the sound of a dull, heavy roar in the distance, and a moment's reflection told us that we were nearing Niagara! And, as the first streaks of sun-light gilded the Eastern horizon, the train slowed up at the end of Suspension Bridge on the Canada side, and we were in plain view and hearing of the great Cataract! I will not attempt to describe the magnificent grandeur of the scene, for a host of writers, in comparison to whom, in regard to descriptive talent, I am as a fire-fly to a sheet of lightning, have fallen far short of the reality. It will suffice to say: The World has thousands of Water-falls, many Cascades, and a few Cataracts—but the World has but ONE NIAGARA!

At this great watering place I tarried for an entire day, vainly trying to drink in the wonderful beauty of the scene; but the longer I remained and the more I looked, the more I realized my inability to grasp the full measure of its fascinating power. In all my wanderings nothing has impressed me so forcibly or filled my mind with a sense of its awe-inspiring sublimity as did the great Falls of Niagara.

Leaving the Falls a little before dark, we were soon traversing the great state of New York, and in the morning arrived at Albany, where after a short stop for breakfast, we were once more on our way, winding along the storied shores of the noble Hudson river. It was Sunday, and although the day was stormy, raining and snowing alternately, the journey was highly enjoyed, the picturesque scenery adorning the banks of this magnificent river, forming a continuous panorama of rare beauty, unrivaled on this continent. Although West Point lay upon the opposite side of the river, we got a pretty good view of the famous old town, so memorably associated with the early history of our country.

It will here be in order to state, that between Peoria and New York, I fell in with seven men who were enroute for California. Some were going for health, some for wealth and some for climate—all hoping and expecting to better their condition. For convenience sake, I will name them Jones, Brown, Jenkins and Ridley, of Illinois; Tripp and German, of Canada, and Olsen, a Norwegian sailor. We were a party of eight individuals whose generel ideas seemed to run in the same direction. While on the cars we had formed a general acquaintance, and solemnly declared that come what would in the future, we would travel together, put up at the same hotel, work together, divide our wages equally, marry the same woman, and if necessary—die together! Of course we all stuck to the agreement, (but it is quite probable that we did nothing of the kind).

About four o'clock on the evening of the 11th, we reached New York City, which, by the way, I found to be a little the biggest institution in the shape of a town that I had ever been in, to the best of my recollection.

As might have been expected, the vast crowd at the depot seemed very glad and also greatly surprized to see us—especially on Sunday (and it a raining, too). It did seem as if all creation wanted us to stay all night with them; but as there were not enough of us to go around, and give every "runner" a show, we declined many pressing invitations; and finally, by what now seems to me a miraculous streak of luck, we stumbled into French's Hotel. (I will here say that at that time, Mr. French appeared to be as fine

a man as one might 'jump up' in any country—
and evidently knew how to keep hotel).

On the morning after our arrival in the City,
while standing on the steps in front of the hotel,
Jenkins, (of Illinois) loaned a mild-eyed stranger
one hundred dollars "just for an hour or so—until the bank opened." Brother Jenkins and the
man with the mild eye never met again in this
cold world.

An hour or so after this sad occurrence, fearing
lest other similar calamities might befall more or
less of our number, we concluded that it would
be policy to go at once and secure our tickets; for
business is business, you know; in fact, business
is one thing and loaning money to a stranger on
a short acquaintance is another thing.

Repairing to the office of the California Mail
Steamship Line, we found the berths all taken,
so we then concluded to wait for a ship of "Rob-
erts' Opposition Line," which was advertised to
leave on the 23rd, and as we were compelled to
remain so long in the great metropolis, in order
to economize, we purchased tickets for the 'Steerage' (for particulars see Webster's unabridged).
During our sojourn in New York, we endeavored to "take in" every place of interest; and it is
needless to add that in nine cases out of ten, it
was that crowd of eight inquiring souls that were
taken in. We traversed Broadway from one end

to the other, also a great many other ways not
quite so broad. We visited Brooklyn, Jersey City, Hobokin, Blackwell's Island, the Navy Yard,
Central Park, Barnum's Museum, and many other points of interest; and finally, when the morning of the 23rd came around, we settled our hotel "williams," shouldered our "traps" and went
on board the old Steam-ship, "Illinois"—bound
for Aspinwall.

"Our Ship is ready, and the wind is fair—
I'm bound for the sea, Mary Ann."

FROM NEW YORK TO ASPINWALL.

At noon the ship's cannon was fired, and a few minutes later the great paddles began to revolve and we were drifting from the shores of America.

There were nearly fifteen hundred passengers on board, about six hundred Irish and the balance from almost every other portion of the civilized world. Every available part of the ship was crowded with humanity, clothed in almost every imaginable garb.

Now, reader, come and cross the big w a t e r with me. Let us sit down in the fore-castle and journalize a little as we steam for the Isthmus.

The waters widen around our ship!

"Adieu, adieu, my native shore
Fades over the waters blue."

The loved land of our nativity grows dim in the distance—the shore is out of sight! The ship goes bounding up and down in a manner not entirely satisfactory to "yours truly." (I wonder if this vessel was duly inspected before she left the harbor). The loud roar and crash of the huge waves as they strike the sides of the ship makes me feel like abandoning all my sinful habits.

APRIL 25. A heavy sea; the waves are rolling
clear over the decks, yet I am not frightened, but
nearly scared to death. The vessel groans as if
she would come to pieces; and if she does I hope
she will come to some good firm pieces of land,
for I feel just now like going into the real estate
business. (An hour later, I changed my mind
and concluded to 'cast my bread upon the waters')

APRIL 26. If I ever do reach California, my
travels on the ocean will be ended.

APRIL 27. Nearly all our "mess" are sick—
awful sick. Dinner is under way. It commences
at noon and lasts until 4 p. m., then supper begins, and that never ends—that is, hardly ever;
at least, that is what a woman passenger said, and
I will not dispute with a woman. Ancient history intimates that I used to do the like when I
was a youth; but hazel switches, promptly administered, taught me lessons, wise, likewise and
otherwise. (I am no youth at this writing).

APRIL 30. In sight of the island of Cuba. It
looks like a gray cloud, stretching along the horizon, but upon a nearer approach it presents bold
shores, the face of the country appearing rather
mountainous, and is interspersed with hills and
valleys dotted with beautiful groves. It was here
that Dr. Kane breathed out the last hours of a
useful life. After his near association with the

grim monster during two dark winters amid the
ice-fields of the Polar regions, it is cheering to
know that the brave explorer was at last permitted to lie down and sleep his last sleep in the
"Queen of Isles," the spot coveted by all nations
—peerless Cuba: where the fragrance of rare spi-
ces and bright flowers fill the air with sweet
perfume.

MAY 3. There is some prospect of reaching
the Isthmus to-night. But little air is stirring
and the weather is oppressively warm. Our ship
represents a full-fledged menagerie. Human nature is here in all its varied forms, and what P.
T. Barnum was doing when we left New York,
is indeed a mystery. He missed an opportunity
for securing a rare collection that may never oc-
cur again.

MAY 4. We arrived at Aspinwall last night
about midnight, and this morning I went up on
deck and got my first view of the "deathly Isthmus." During our voyage to this place, owing to
the crowded vessel, the passengers generally, considered that they had been very badly treated by
the ship's company, in regard to the scanty supply of water, poor rations, &c. These complaints
were especially loud in the steerage department;
and about fifteen committees had been organi-
zed to lay our common grievances before the

American Consul upon our arrival at Aspinwall. It was understood that just as soon as the complaint was made, the Consul would immediately put the ship's officers in irons and give every passenger about ten dollars to patch up their outraged feelings. Day after day these special committees wended their way to the residence of the Consul, and day after day that official put them off promising to attend to the matter soon as he could "get to it." It is needless to say that the dear old Consul never got there.

The natives of both sexes come in crowds to the wharf with baskets of their own peculiar fashioning, laden with tempting fruit, sea shells, &c.

The principal production of industry at this place, and apparently the chief article for sale at the mercantile establishments appears to be Jamaica Rum, and I regret to say that about one-third of our male passengers, in their frequent and continued wrestling with this powerful adversary, became what may very appropriately be termed "total wrecks."

Many of the natives go around dressed decidedly "seldom," and live chiefly upon the natural products of the country. They lead an indolent life, and spend much of their time laying in the shade, swinging in hammocks and dancing; and to all appearances enjoy life far better than more civilized races. They have nothing to worry their

minds about, for upon every hand they see a
bountiful harvest, spread out by the lavish hand
of Nature. What's the use of working in a land
like this? If the climate was healthy for the
white race it could easily be converted into an
earthly paradise; but fierce disease and threat-
ening death keep back the wheels of civilization.

We boarded the train and left Aspinwall on
the 6th. The country across the Isthmus, a distance of forty-six miles, as I viewed it from the
car window, seemed to be a mixture of the beautiful, wonderful, grand, gloomy and peculiar; the
face of the country growing much higher
as we approach Panama. We passed several vil-
lages along the way, peopled entirely by natives.
Their houses are built of a kind of bamboo, cane
and palm, neatly thatched, and are all well ven-
tilated.

Before leaving Aspinwall, Jones and I laid in
half a gallon of Jamaica rum to keep the mosquitoes from biting us,)mosquitoes grow unusu-

ally large, and are very vicious in Central America), and as snakes in this country also grow to an enormous size and are exceedingly venomous, Ridley and Brown laid in half a gallon of Jamaica's "boss wrestler" to keep off the snakes. It is needless to add that during the remainder of the journey we were not molested, either by mosquitoes or snakes.

We arrived at Panama in the afternoon, and found the connecting steamer, "Moses Taylor," waiting for us; and such a time as we had getting on board simply beggars description. We had to go out quite a distance in small boats and climb up to the decks on a ladder. Every body wanted to go first (they were afraid of getting left, and I am sorry we wasn't). There was pushing, jamming, crowding, swearing, and occasionally fighting; and it was all the ship's officers could do to keep the boats from being swamped by the impatient crowd. That crowd was composed of people from nearly every civilized country—from nearly every station in life—*civilized people!* They knew we were all going—knew the ship was large enough to carry all of us, and also knew it would wait for us. It was then, and is yet my opinion, that rum was at the bottom of all this trouble. The improper use of intoxicating liquors certainly destroys all that is good and noble in the heart of man (or woman either), or any other man, or any of his relatives; but for all this, I suppose strong drink will be bought, sold and drank; and men will crowd, push, quarrel and fight just as long as—as long as snakes and mosquitoes threaten to bite travelers.

MAY 11. This morning a little before daylight the 'Moses Taylor' got up steam and 'stood' for San Francisco. The land has once more faded from our sight, and the blue waters of the Pacific ocean form the horizon on every side. Dinner is under way, and the order of the hour seems to be to pitch in, shove back the women and children, overturn the coffee pots and curse the steward if he is handy.

MAY 12. Last night we boys went below to see if we could find our bunks; after some trouble we found our sleeping apartment located between the engine room and the butcher stalls; of course, we wakened up considerably—did not feel sleepy anyhow, so up we came and turned in on deck in the open air and went to sleep; but during the night the wind arose, the sea grew boisterous and we were awakened by the angry dashing of the waves, and soon a drenching rain came pouring down. The heavens were ablaze with lightning. It was "midnight on the ocean.' I yet remember, as I leaned over the railing, how I shrank back horrified, as I beheld the white-crested waves rolling up within a few feet of me,

splashing the water in my face. The roar of the
waters, the groaning of the vessel, the crashing
of the thunder, and the spectral-like watch in the
forecastle (seen by the lightning's glare), striking the bells for the midnight hour, all had an
effect upon the author.

MAY 13. One of our passengers died last night,
—a young man who was on the road to Oregon
with his newly married wife. It is a sad case.
they are lowering the body over the side of the
ship, and I can hear the Chaplain reading: "I am
the Resurrection and the Life." It seems a fearful thing to be buried at sea.

MAY 18. In sight of the coast of Mexico. The
temperature is getting cooler. This is our seventh
day on the Pacific; and the hours drag slowly by.

> To the West, far out, blue billows roll,
>   As onward swift we go,
> While to the East, in grandeur rise—
>   The cliffs of Mexico.
>
> The mountains dark and grim loom up;
>   Even to the clouds they reach,
> While Cocoa groves in quiet, rest
>   Along the sandy beach.
>
> Tehuantepec's broad gulf we've passed—
>   The sun is sinking low,   ·
> And in the gathering darkness, fades
>   The coast of Mexico.

MAY 20. This is the anniversary of my birth-
day, but I have been too badly frightened during
the past few days to tell exactly how old I am;
however I am positive that I have aged consid-

erably since I left home. The evening is beautiful, and to use the words of a somewhat smarter man than I am: "the sun is going down in a halo of glory." (but I can't help that).

Sun-set on the ocean! What is more glorious? What fills the mind with more impressive emotions? I know what fills my mind with more thrilling emotions than seeing the sun set on the ocean. It is the thought that I may not have the privilege of seeing it rise in the morning!

MAY 23. In sight of Lower California. The head-lands of cape St. Lucas rise in the distance; saw several whales to-day. Lower California presents a desolate appearance—barren hills and desolate wastes. (If "my girl" ever presents as desolate a waist as lower California, I shall never attempt to surround her).

MAY 25. We are nearing California! We passed Monterey about noon. The sailors are getting the cables ready and putting the ship in order. In the distance I can see the ever-green shores of the happy land. Horses, cattle and sheep are grazing on the grassy slopes, and "I long to be there too."

Our grand army of passengers all seem happy at the prospect of soon being on shore. The decks are crowded with men, women and children—enough people to fill up a small town.

Jottings by the way, on the road to California, will soon be laid aside. Yonder is the Golden Gate! Up goes my old hat as the city heaves in view! The sun is setting, and we are passing into the harbor of San Francisco.

I thank the Giver of all good that I have escaped the dangers of the deep and been permitted to witness the sun go down, from the shores of the Pacific ocean.

To our noble Ship, "Moses Taylor," I touch my hat. To ocean life, a long farewell.

California: I stand upon your golden shore.— Your white sands glisten beneath my feet, and your blue sky, studded with brilliant stars, spread out over my head!

LIFE IN CALIFORNIA.

HOW EIGHT PARTNERS STUCK TOGETHER.

Before leaving the steamer, "Moses Taylor," our crowd (the notorious eight) got together and unanimously resolved (according to our previous general arrangement), that we would all go to the same hotel—of course we would; and on the following morning we would settle on plans for the future that would speedily pour shekels into the capacious pockets of the aforesaid eight; and we also remarked: "Woe unto that "runner," who in the blindness of his zeal, undertakes to separate our crowd, for the unfortunate descendant of Adam who should make such an attempt would indeed be fortunate if he escaped great bodily injury, for behold, we are bad medicine to indulge in."

Reader, perhaps you are aware that it was no small job to go ashore from an ocean steamer, after dark, in San Francisco twenty years ago! In those days, aside from Ben Holiday's Stage Line, the bulk of the travel from the 'States' to California was on ocean steamers—by the Panama and Nicaragua routes; and the arrival of a steamer was met by thousands of people, assembled on the piers; and hotel runners in the crowd were far more numerous than snakes and mosquitoes were on the Isthmus. The citizens came to look for relatives and friends; on the night of our arrival, it was evident that the hotel runners came —to look for us. (In the majority of cases I regret to say, they found us).

In regard to going ashore, I will not lacerate the feelings of the reader, by entering too minutely into particulars, but will venture the statement, that it took just seven hotels to accommodate our crowd of eight! Jenkins and I fell into the clutches of a human porcupine, who r e p r e-sented the old 'St. Louis' hotel, down on Pacific street—although we did not discover each other's whereabouts until we accidentally met the next morning in the dining room. The other six members of our "mess" were coaxed, pulled, jerked, kidnapped, and scattered promiscuously almost from the old "Barbary coast" to the Cliff House: and it took close searching, the greater portion of the next day to get us all together. But, alas! It was then too late. The "bonds of partnership" had been loosened—the mischief had been done. Each one of our party had swallowed his little dose of instructions, gratuitously administered, by the fatherly advisors, who infested the city, and who, I may add, can be found everywhere; and after this, with our crowd, calm reasoning found no willing ears.

In the city we found plenty of men who "knew all about California and the whole Pacific coast," and their experience and advice reminded me of streams of lava emitted from Mt. Vesuvius.

One man said: "Go to the old mines of California, that's whar I made my 'raise' in '52." (this individual at this time was lunching at a "free soup house" on the proceeds of his "raise." Another man said: "Stranger, if you want to pick up chunks of coarse gold like a duck picks up corn, you go to Arizona." "But," said one of our crowd, "why don't you go there?" The reply was, "It costs one hundred dollars to go there, and I have only four bits to start on.")

Another miserable specimen of American humanity advised us to go to Alaska and engage in the fur business; but we concluded that Alaska was a little too "fur" off.

I was also advised to buy a quartz mill and go to Nevada and try my hand at crushing rock— "for," said my sage advisor, "there is millions in it." As this venture took nearly a million to start it, I concluded to let the quartz mill alone, at least for a week or two.

To make a long story short, it will be sufficient to say, that upon the third day after our arrival in San Francisco, we (our crowd of eight) indulged in a general leave-taking of each other, each one promising, in case he "struck it rich" to notify the other boys "right off." (I for one, have not yet been notified.)

While on the steamer, Jones had become acquainted with a young lady, and this young lady was going to Sacramento; and Jones concluded that Sacramento was good enough for him, and he went—and I saw him no more.

Brown and Ridley went over to Oakland to hunt up an old friend; and although more than twenty years have elapsed since then, I do not yet know whether they found that friend or not.

German and Tripp went to Benicia, stayed a few weeks and then "lit out" for Canada.

Jenkins went to Petaluma, and from there to Sebastopol, and from there to Illinois, and from there back to California, and from there to old Missouri—(and that nearly let him out),—and from there back to California, where he became a financial wreck—a true representative of what I term—Hungry Land.

Olsen, the old sailor, secured a job at washing dishes at a hotel in the city, for his board; but I afterwards learned that a test trial of one week ended the contract, bankrupting the hotel keeper, and forcing Olsen into the hospital, where he lay for seven weeks under treatment for the gout! It was no fair test, as Olsen had just came off a long ocean voyage, and steerage fare no doubt had a tendency to "scuttle" his earthly tabernacle to some extent. If that hotel keeper, by mortgaging his furniture, could have managed to keep his table going for one week longer, I think the old sailor might have filled up and toned down to business—but, such is life.

I had several inducements offered me in the way of employment. One man from the "upper country" offered me forty dollars per month, and he said all I had to do was to milk twenty cows before breakfast, curry off seventeen horses, then do up the chores, and put in the balance of the time in the field. I told him I would "see him again," but I was very careful not to name any particular time or place; and when I did see him again, I took particular care to know that he did not see me. Finally, I went up to Sonoma county, and took a job of chopping cord-wood, in the vicinity of Petaluma, and no doubt I would have continued at it until this day, had I not commenced thinking, how it would mar the beauty of the landscape to have all the trees cut down! That settled me. I did not wish to spoil a country with "my little hatchet" I love fine scenery, so I

threw up the job and went up on Russian river,
near where the town of Guerneville now stands
(in Pocket canyon), and sat down in the shade of
a huge Redwood tree, and went to shaving shingles.

Thus, you see, kind reader, we are creatures of
circumstances; and although it is an easy thing
for any one to look back and see where opportunities were missed, and to see where we might
have done different; but it is not such an easy
task to look forward and see what is best for us
to do, and figure out the results of the future.

Of our crowd of eight persons, in coming to
California, perhaps not one of us ever realized our
cherished expectations. No doubt all left home,
full of hope, inter-woven with the glowing antici-
pations of an improved and prosperous future—
and no doubt every one of us, upon our arrival
here, accepted situations, which, had the same
been tendered us back home, would have been
indignantly refused. I could have got plenty of
wood to chop in Illinois, but the axe at "our old
wood-pile" did not suit me; and it is quite likely
that a similar illustration could be applied to all
the other boys.

It is a note-worthy fact that a great many individuals ramble through life, until they are almost ready to die, before the bitter lessons of experience assert their supremacy, and show them

how to live. As Shakespeare truly said, it is

Better to bear the ills we have, than fly to those we know not of.

Reader, if there is a spot on this earth—be it ever so small—a place that you can call HOME— no matter whether it is in the ice-clad regions of the North, or beneath the dreamy skies of the "Sun-lands"—my advice to you—first, last, and all the time, is:—*be contented, and stay there.*

With a *Home* and *Friends*—and a *Contented mind*, the World is beautiful almost anywhere; and without these jewels, you will find the world a barren, cheerless waste—a *hungry land*, no matter where you go.

Those earthly jewels:—a Home, Friends, and Contentment are within the reach of almost every one. The first may be gained by Industry, Economy and Sobriety; the second may be secured by Honesty and upright dealing; and Contentment will come of itself, and abide with us, if we take the right view of Life, for—

"Life is short, and Time is fleeting—
And our hearts, though stout and brave,
Still, like muffled drums are beating,
Funeral marches to the grave."

FOOD FOR REFLECTION.

We are marching on—There is no resting place this side the grave.—With many of us the meridian is passed—the dew-drops that sparkled and glistened on the roses that bloomed in our morning have long since melted away beneath the scorching rays of the noon-day sun. We are writing history.—Our epitaphs will soon be read on Time's ledger, wherein are inscribed those acts, be they good or evil, that never die. Do we realize this? Do we ever stop to think how much good *can be done*, and how little *is done*, according to our opportunities? If we would all do the best we can, we would soon have a society that would unlock the prison doors, snatch the victim from the scaffold—reclaim the drunkard—and bring heaven almost to earth!

There are none too puny, and none too weak to make gallant soldiers, and win unfading laurels in battling for the Right.

THE STORY OF A MILLION.

(The following little parody I wrote and sent to my brothers in Mason City, Illinois, in the winter of 1864, after having had a little experience among the old miners on Yuba River).

Ho! ye people from afar off:
Ye who live beyond the mountains,
Far beyond the Rocky mountains,
Far beyond the yellow waters
Of the mighty Mississippi!
Ye who live in Mason City—
Come and listen to my story;
Rally 'round, and get up closer—
Closer, so you'll hear the story,
Of my long and weary journey—
Of my journey to this country,
To this far-off western country,
To the land of California.

How I started off that morning—
On that mild and bright Spring morning!
How I heard the wild birds singing,
How I watched the village fading—
Fading out so far behind me;
Heard the hum of distant voices,
Die upon my ear so sadly,
How I met with other travelers—
Travelers bound for California.

How we started, and kept on going,
Going on our distant journey,
To the pleasant land of sunshine—
To the land of California.

How we reached the bustling city,
The dashing city on the lake-shore—
The giant city of Chicago;
How we tried to eat our breakfast,
Tried to throw ourselves outside it,
Tried it hard, but could not do it,
Because the cars were in a hurry;
How we jumped on board so quickly,
And started on for California.

How we reached Detroit at sun-set—
Reached there, oh, so very hungry;
How we went on board the ferry,
How we tried to get our supper,
How we sat down to the table,
How we paid our money for it.
How we paid a half a dollar,
Just to get a cup of coffee:
How we sat and kept a looking—
Looking for that cup of coffee,
Looked and looked, yet could not see it.

How we crossed the Detroit river,
Into Canada how we crossed o'er,
Where they said the cars were waiting.
Waiting for us hungry people;
How we got on board and started,
On our journey, oh so sleepy,
On our journey, oh, so hungry—
On the road to California.

But it soon set in to raining,
Raining hard and raining steady—
Steady 'cause it kept on raining.
Thus the night wore on so dreary,
Sometimes we sang and oft-times nodded,
Nodded at the folks all 'round us,
And they, to keep the thing a going,
Nodded back, all through politeness.
But we found 'twould soon be morning,
Found that day-light was approaching,
Found that we were nearing somewhere,
Found the cars were going slower,
Heard the locomotive whistle,
Then it was we heard a roaring,
Heard a sound like distant thunder,
Like the roar of mighty waters,
Like a coming storm we heard it;
Then the truth burst in upon us—
We were nearing Niagara—
The mighty Falls of Niagara!
Soon we 'gan to cross the river,
On the wire bridge, Suspension,
Stretched across the rushing torrent;
Then it was I saw the waters,
Pouring over Niagara,
Saw the spray rise up so grandly—
Even to the clouds it rose up,
Forming bows of many colors
And the noise—oh, it was deafening!
As I write, methinks I hear it:—
Hear the roar, the deafening thunder,
Of the mighty Niagara.
Oh! I wish that I could tell you,

Tell you everything I thought of,
Tell you what my mind was filled with.
Tell you how my heart it rose up—
Rose up 'til I could not say it;
 I could tell you all about it,
If I was in Mason City—
All about our journey onward,
All about the lovely scenery,
That we saw upon our journey,
How we crossed o'er running streamlets,
How we ran through gloomy tunnels,
Then along the edge of hill-tops,
How we traveled on for hours,
Along the banks of Hudson river,
 When we arrived in New York City,
'Twas on a rainy Sunday evening;
And the folks there did not know us!
Did not know us, 'cause we'd grown so,
Because we came so unexpected.
 For three weeks we there did tarry,
Tarried there in New York City,
Stayed there 'til our ship was ready,
Then we got on board and started—
Started on our ocean voyage;
Soon the river 'gan to widen,
Began to widen into ocean.
 Then our hearts grew sad within us,
When we saw the shores receding,
When we saw the city fading—
Fading farther in the distance—
Saw the waters widen 'round us.
Saw the great big waves dash by us,
And knew they were not from the river.

Knew that we were on the waters
Of the broad Atlantic ocean.
I could tell of strange proceedings
That took place upon the steamer,
And what I saw upon the voyage,
But I know 'twould tire your patience,
So I will hurry on the journey,
Hurry over the Atlantic,
Hurry by the lovely islands,
Hurry o'er the "deathly Isthmus,"
Where the birds of brilliant plumage
There do sing their songs so sweetly;
Where the Palm trees rise so graceful;
Where Cocoa nuts and ripe Bananas
Hang in clusters all around you;
Where the natives dress so oddly,
Where they sing and dance so wildly,
Where the monkeys "cut such capers"
As I'm certain would surprise you.
I will not attempt to tell you,
Of our second ocean voyage,
On Pacific's mighty billows;
Until we got to San Francisco—
To the end of our long journey,
To the land of California.
But, methinks I hear you asking—
Asking me to stop and tell you
How I like this western country—
What I think of California!
I will answer, I will tell you,
Tell you all I know about it,
Tell you why most people come here,
Why they leave their homes behind them,
Why they come to California.

Many come with expectations,
Come with mighty expectations,
Come to get rich, oh, so quickly,
Come to get rich, so immensely—
Come to get rich, in a hurry,
Come to get the "almighty dollar."

Many come and go to mining—
Digging for the precious metal,
Labor hard, and live much harder—
Almost live on what's called nothing,
All for the "almighty dollar;"
And many there are who do not find it,
Hunt for years and do not find it,
Dig and look, but cannot "see it;"
Then they get so disappointed—
Get so awfully discouraged,
Because they cannot find the dollar,
The great big California dollar;
The dollar they so oft have heard of,
The dollar they so oft have dreamed of,
The dollar which they all expected!
The dollar that they sold their farms for,
The dollar that is always brightest
When seen at the greatest distance;
The dollar that beats all creation,
The dollar that defies description,
The dollar of hallucination—
The dollar of imagination!

Very brightly shines that dollar,
When you see it from afar off;
But the nearer you approach it:
Its great proportions 'gin to lessen;

Then your heart it sinks within you,
Then you begin to get so home-sick,
Begin to think you've acted foolish,
Begin to wish you had not started,
Begin to wish you was 'most nowhere,
Begin to smell the wolf, "starvation"—
The gaunt and hungry wolf, "starvation."

You can hear him growl behind you,
You can hear him bark before you,
You can hear him whine beside you—
See him walk in circles 'round you—
Feel that soon he'll be upon you,
If you do not find the dollar;
But the dollar begins to lessen,
Begins to lose its great proportions,
About the time you get *close to it*;
Thus it is with many miners,
In the land of California.

Then they begin to grow most reckless,
Begin to curse the "golden country,"
Begin to wish they all had perished,
On the road to California!

Then begins their life of roving—
Roving through the mountain gulches,
Roving through the gloomy canyons,
In search for the "almighty dollar;"
But some there are who have been lucky,
In their searches for the treasure;
But this I say: (for Truth is mighty),

Of all the mighty emigration
That have rushed to California:—
They who came from every nation:—

From the sunny dales of England,
From fair Scotland's hills of heather,
From the vineyards of the Frenchmen,
From the Italian's land so lovely,
From the mighty walls of China,
From the gold-fields of Australia,
From the islands of the ocean,
From every State in our old Union,
From the snow-clad Russian Empire,
From every hill and plain and valley,
From every city, town and hamlet—
(For all are here in California):
Few there are that ever find it—
Ever find *just what they came for*,
In the land of California!

There is many a sad, sad story,
Many a story of the starting,
Many a story of the coming,
Many a broken-hearted story,
Many a wretched miner's story,
Many a story that would grieve you,
Many a story that would pain you—
Pain you at its sad recital;
Stories *started*, *wrote* and *finished*,
By the trip to California!

But methinks I hear you asking,
What about this matchless climate?
I will answer, I will tell you—
Tell you all I know about it.
There is much that's very pleasant,
In the Summer, Spring and Autumn;
For the sun it shines out brightly,
For eight months it shines out brightly,

And the breezes blow so softly,
From the great Pacific ocean;
Then comes on the rainy season,
Sometimes raining 'most all winter,
Sometimes raining, sometimes ceasing,
Ceasing only to renew it,
Through the California winter.

Some say people never die here,
Never die, but live forever;
But I say, they are mistaken,
For 'tis here the same as elsewhere.
People, they get sick and die here,
Die because they cannot help it,
Die, and start off on that journey,
On that dark, uncertain journey,
To that land beyond the river,
To the land of the "Hereafter."

They leave this land of sunny climate,
Leave this land of lovely valleys,
Leave the grand old mountain ranges,
Leave this land so full of beauty—
Leave the new-found paying diggings,
Look no more for gold and silver,
No more for the "almighty dollar,"
Look their last on all things earthly,
Leave all behind—and in the leaving—
Leave the land of California!

Such is Life, as I have found it;
Such is Life, this wide world over;
Life is short, and Death is certain,
On the land or on the ocean—
And 'tis the same in California.

Brothers, my task is almost finished,
My story is almost completed.
I pray that some day I may meet you—
Meet you far beyond the mountains,
Far beyond the sandy deserts,
Far beyond the big Platte river,
Far beyond the yellow waters
Of the mighty Mississippi;
In the loved land of my boy-hood,
In the land of youth's sweet spring-time.
In the land of golden memories—
Of fond and cherished recollections—
There is where I hope to meet you.

Will you there, await my coming,
With loving hearts, await my coming,
When I bid good-bye to mining,
Good-bye to this Western country—
A long good-bye to California?

PILGRIMS ON THE TRAMP.

THE Autumn of 1864 found me once more in the wood chopping business, this time, near the old town of Sebastopol, Sonoma county. In the meantime I had formed the acquaintance of a blacksmith named Reed, and he and I resolved to "stick together." At the time my story opens, we were both doing very well, considering our respective avocations:—each one laying up his little dollar-and-a-half every now and then—yet, like the average specimens of advanced civilization, we both felt quite sure that we could do a great deal better "somewhere else," and we were contemplating a trip to pastures new and fields more green: In short, we informed our friends that it was our intention to hunt *a better climate and more money.*

We met one evening in the village shoe shop, to decide the question as to where we should go and when we should start.

Arizona, New Mexico and Montana were talked of; but Reed had his head set for the old mines of California. He knew there was money there; he had been there in '52, made a lucky "strike" and then struck for home, bought a farm in Iowa and settled down; but visions of old haunted his brain, and *unsettled* him, and here he was again in California. After a heated discussion regarding the different points, we finally agreed to let luck point out our road to fortune, which now lay between Arizona and the old mines of California.

Into Reed's hat went three Nevada "quarters" "Give her a shake, Reed," said I. Up came Arizona. "Try it again, old man." This time it was in Reed's favor. "Hurrah for the old mines, there is money there," shouted Reed, greatly excited. The last shake however, favored Arizona, and that point was settled.

"Hurrah for Arizona!" we both shouted; "Let the Apaches and Commanches sound their war whoop; Reed and the wood-cutter are coming down among you, and—women, children and very old men had better get out of the way."

We began at once to get ready for the tramp, in a leisurely sort of way, the greater portion of two days being consumed in packing our valises, the contents of which, all told, would not have footed up a cash value of more than seven dollars; and then we bid good-bye to everything in the shape of sympathetic human nature in that neighborhood, and departed for San Francisco.

That was in the early part of November and we thought we could reach the gold fields before the rainy season commenced.

While on our way to San Francisco, on the steamer we met a Sonoma county ranchman named Jones, whom we knew to be one of the wealthiest men in the county. We told him we were enroute for Arizona; but he had no faith in the lower country, but said he could put us on the track of something better in the old mines of California. He told us of a certain bar on the North Fork of Yuba river, where himself and a partner had kept a boarding house and a trading store in '49, dealing out provisions, etc., to the miners of that region; and one day, while at that place, he and his partner were putting up a new boarding tent, and digging down the river bank to make it level they discovered a decomposed quartz ledge that was literally full of coarse gold, but as they were making money faster and easier than by digging for it, they carefully covered it up, hammered down the dirt, and erected their tent over the place, and Jones said he was satisfied everything (except the tent) was still there, just as they had left it sixteen years ago, and if we wished to unearth it, all we had to do was to go up there and—dig. He felt satisfied it would pay us much better than anything in the savage regions of Arizona. We concluded to study about it, and the more we studied, the wilder Arizona looked; and I am sorry to say, that by the time we arrived in San Francisco, it was whispered through the crowd on the pier that we looked rather wild ourselves. However, after a brief consultation we concluded to visit the Yuba river country and hunt up that quartz ledge or "bust." That night we put up at what was then known as the Chicago Hotel, on Pacific street. There I met Olsen, the old Norwegian sailor. He was glad to see me, poor fellow; he had been sick—a stranger in a strange land. He had recently got news from Norway,—his only brother had lately died and his sweetheart had married a better looking man than he was. As he told me his sad story, his eyes filled with tears, and in his broken English begged me to be a brother to him —he wanted to call somebody a friend, for to him the world seemed wide and desolate. I promised him everything (but money). I told him I would be a brother to him and a sister also, if I only dared to. I could well afford to be generous, as Reed and I were going to the "old mines."

While we were in San Francisco, we fell in with a man who we will call "Jeems." This man "Jeems" had an honest face, and wished to try his luck in the mines; so we concluded to take him in as a partner (he was badly taken in); so after taking a "bird's eye" view of San Francisco, we went on board a steamboat, bound for Marysville, where we arrived in due season.

We tarried over night in Marysville, and on the following morning we purchased a frying-pan and coffee-pot, and a few of the necessaries of life, and set out upon our journey. After a hard day's tramp, supposing that we had traveled at least forty miles, about sun-down we came to Brown's Valley, a small mining town, and a sign board loomed up with a finger pointing to the figures: "Marysville, 11 miles." No matter, we were tired and after passing through the village, we "went into camp," which means to say: we kindled a fire, made about three gallons of coffee, drank it and then curled up under a tree and passed our first night in the gold mining region of California! There was exhileration in the thought!

On the following morning we started for the old town of French Corral, situated on what in early days was known as the "Henness Pass" Route, where we arrived about four o'clock in the afternoon, and stopped a short time at a way-side Inn kept by an old man named Browning, who had lived in that vicinity for several years.

After refreshing the 'inner man,' we consulted our rudely drawn maps, and became satisfied that we were in the immediate vicinity of the bar that contained the hidden ledge; and after gaining all the information we could from Browning, in regard to the country, we struck out on a rude trail leading up the river, Mr. Browning having informed us that it was his opinion that the bar we were in search of, was at that time known as "Condemned Bar."

A short time before sun-down, we reached the Bar, and found ourselves in one of the gloomiest places imaginable. The mountain tops seemed to almost meet, as they hung frowning over us on each side of the river. A deep ravine came down at the upper end of the bar; and we found the place in possession of several Chinamen, who were engaged in mining with "rockers" along the banks of the river. Altogether, it was decidedly a hard looking place.

The Chinamen seemed rather unsociable, and evidently regarded our coming as an encroachment upon their rights as "old settlers," and several times during the evening, the following confab ensued between us:

Chinamen.—"You come here to-day—you go 'way all same to-morrow?

Our crowd.—"Melican men come to dig up this bar—find big ledge—make lots of money—hire Chinamen to shovel heap dirt—give him six bits a day. After while you go back to China, very rich man."

During the evening, I asked Reed how he liked the "old mines." He simply answered: "I have a farm in Iowa, and "I long to be there, too."

I then turned to our companion, "Jeems," and

asked him how he liked the situation; and I felt
sorry for him as he turned his honest face to me
and said: " I've got a sweetheart in Iowa; I am
engaged to her but I'd give one hundred dollars
to be released from her to-night." He, like the
rest of us, was getting very homesick and lone-
some in this gloomy place; I told Jeems if he'd
stay one week on that bar and then have his picture taken and send it to his girl I thought that
considerable less than one hundred dollars would
let him off. We were in a lonely place and did
not like the looks of our neighbors. So after
supper, we sat around our camp-fire forming our
plans, and occasionally firing our revolvers over
the Chinamen's cabin; this we did to let them
know that we were a very dangerous set of men
and not to be trifled with.

About midnight we were awakened by a roaring, crackling noise, and springing to our feet,
we discovered the surprising fact that we had
kindled our fire near the edge of a deep "shaft,"
that had doubtless been sunk many years before
for mining purposes. This shaft had been filled
up with drift-wood and other debris, which was
dry as tinder, and our camp-fire had ignited the
(w)hole. We had scarcely time to remove our bed-
ding (which, owing to a scarcity, all we had to do
was to crawl off), when the flames shot up fully
fifty feet. Reed guessed the height of the flames

at fifty-one feet, and Jeems insisted on fifty-one feet and four inches; but I am willing to adhere to my first proposition, and call it fifty feet.

It was an exciting time for a few minutes.— Reed fired off his old "navy" and shrieked: "To arms!" And Jeems and I rushed frantically into his arms. The panic stricken Chinamen came dashing out of their shanty with about a nickle's worth of second hand clothing on the whole lot, and a short time after, a few plunges and blind splashes was sufficient proof to us that our neighbors had crossed the Yuba.

During the night, the heavens were obscured by heavy clouds, and a little before daylight we were roused from our slumbers by the rain pouring down with a steady measure that plainly indicated the first storm of the winter.

We held a brief consultation. The big shaft, that was still belching up flames and smoke, indicated that the bar had been prospected; we also had learned from Mr. Browning that the original beds of nearly all the mining streams in that vicinity lay buried all the way from forty to sixty feet below their present surface, the streams having been filled up with "tailings" "sluiced" down from the hills above; and we also argued that we might not be on the right bar after all; and, with a driving storm howling over us, we made up our minds to go down the mount-

ains and try our luck in the foot-hills, nearer a
base for supplies—and then, if nothing better
presented itself, we would go back to Sonoma
county, see Jones and get a more complete description of the bar, and try it again some other
day, earlier in the season.

After a hurried breakfast, in which crackers
played a conspicuous part, we took the trail to
Browning's, where we arrived about three o'clock
in the afternoon, very tired after toiling over the
most narrow and by far the most slippery trail I
ever traveled—said trail, the greater portion of
the way (about seven miles), winding along the
mountains' side, overlooking the river—sometimes mid-way between the bed of the stream and
the mountains' rocky crest.

While we were engaged in drying our rain
drenched garments, and warming ourselves up
by the different processes known to western travelers, a heavy train, loaded with machinery for
a quartz mill, drawn by oxen, came along—enroute for Egan's Canyon. The proprietor of this
train wanted a few more ox drivers and as we
considered ourselves sharp enough to drive, we
resolved to apply for a situation. It was agreed
that I should do the talking, showing forth our
qualifications etc., and Reed and Jeems were to
endorse everything I said. I said to much. I
told the train master, that in regard to Jeems'

qualifications as an ox driver, I really knew nothing, but if the way he handled beef around the camp-fire was any recommendation, he certainly had no equal in the western country. I then launched off in a general way on the peculiar manner in which Reed and I had of driving affairs—told the train-master that we had done the principal portion of our traveling with a pair of *calves*, and if we could not drive *oxen*, it was no fault of ours.

After a short consultation with the teamsters, it was agreed by us to test our qualifications for handling an ox whip. Reed tried his hand first. Taking the 'gad' in his hands, near the butt end, he whirled the heavy lash furiously over his head for a few moments, and then bracing his feet and assuming the form of a crescent, he blazed away at the nearest ox, but instead of striking the animal, he cut a gash fully 4 feet long in the canvas sheet that covered the train-master's wagon.— Reed went into Browning's bar-room to get some change. My turn came next. I caught hold of the whip-stock about the middle, gave the lash a vigorous whirl, "whaled" away and succeeded in throwing a lasso-like noose around the neck of the train-master, who happened to stand too near the chap from Illinois. Of course we adjourned to Browning's front room, and for a few minutes money was no object to me. In regard to the ox-driving profession, Reed and I were excused, and Jeems was offered $30 a month and board, to drive to Egan's Canyon, with the understanding, that after he arrived there, he was to have work in the mines at higher wages; he was determined to get back to Iowa, and thinking this a move in the right direction, he accepted the situation, and the train moved on.

The dark gloom of winter was already lowering over the rugged steeps of the Sierras, and to reach Egan's Canyon would require several weeks of travel and deprivation, through a wild and uninhabited region, amid terrible storms— the recollections of which, even yet, causes many of the old settlers of the Pacific coast to shudder. At this writing, memory points to a picture, not unmingled with sadness:—It was Jeems' last view of his quartz hunting companions—Reed and I. As he reached the first bend in the road, above us, he turned around, swung his hat above his head, and shouted: "Good-bye boys," and a few moments later, Jeems was one of the friends we had seen, but beheld no more. The sad sound of his voice—his last good-bye, like many others, has followed me with its mournful echo through the shadowy mists of years.

That night we camped in Browning's bar-room. Browning was an old bachelor, and had no housekeeper, but he kept an assortment of "fluid extracts" that seemed to obviate all necessity for extra help. One of his hands had been "chawed" off by a grizzly bear; and he interested us until a late hour with thrilling sketches connected with his life in the Sierras.

Very early the next morning, I awoke and discovered my worthy partner "tending bar" all by himself. Of course I asked him why such things were 'thusly,' and he replied that he was "merely taking an invoice of Browning's stock on hand.' As I was out of employment, and a long distance from home, I immediately applied for a position as book-keeper or something of the kind; but before any definite conclusion had been arrived at, old brother Browning came in, and your humble servant swiftly hid himself beneath his pair of "second-hand" blankets and snored; but from my humble couch I heard Browning telling Reed that he would "treat," give us our breakfast and pay our way to Marysville, if we would push out that morning. Reed—with an eye to business, told him if he would throw in two tin cups and three 14 inch plugs of tobacco, the proposition would be accepted. The trade was closed without further parley. An hour later, we shouldered our valises, and with a miserable attempt to inaugurate a camp-meeting, we sang out:

Good-bye, old Browning, stick to your "stand;"
To you and yours, a long adieu;
Old Reed invoiced your stock on hand—
And we are bound for Timbuctoo.

And then we traveled, that is—we trudged.

As we had no old decomposed quartz ledges on hand to bother us, we concluded to strike out for Parks' Bar, on the Yuba river, in the vicinity of Brown's Valley, and try our luck digging in the "old mines." (This was Reed's strong hold).

We reached Park's Bar in due season, and the old man, named Wescott, who kept a toll foot-bridge at that place told us that he had a bank of gravel near by which he considered "pay dirt." We put up nearly our last dollar and bought the claim and commenced getting ready for business.

In the first place, we took possession of an old deserted cabin on the bank of the river: then we borrowed about twenty sluice boxes; we also borrowed enough stove-wood to last us all winter; then we borrowed an old worn out cook-stove—borrowed a sack of flour—in fact, we borrowed everything that could be borrowed in that neighborhood; and then, we twirled our old hats over our heads and shouted: "Let winter storms descend—let loose the flood gates—Reed and his partner are well heeled."

As soon as possible, we placed our sluice boxes into position above the river, with good facilities for 'dumping' into the stream; and then—armed with picks and shovels we went to work.

After keeping our sluice running for two weeks we "cleaned up" and found about fifteen dollars

of the "precious metal," which was amalgamated
by quicksilver, which is used to pick up fine gold,
and this little treasure Reed undertook to retort,
by placing it in an iron shovel and holding it
over the fire—when suddenly the shovel became
red-hot, and our gold disappeared in the shovel
—absorbed! Then it become oppressively apparent that two 'busted' miners stood on the bank
of Yuba river—with

"No one to love, none to caress us."

But we had the best shovel on the bar—there
was money in it—but it was a *borrowed* shovel,
and the owner wanted it.

Again we resumed operations: borrowed more
quicksilver, and made our calculations for another 'clean-up' on a certain Saturday, when sad
to relate, on the Friday previous, a terrible rain
storm set in; Yuba river rose with wonderful rapidity; and on Saturday morning we awoke to
discover that the toll-bridge and all our sluice-
boxes had been swept down the river during the
night—and we never more beheld them!

About this time, we realized that we were a
long way from home—strangers in a strange land
and "flat broke." We had not heard from home
for nearly three months—did not really know
that we had a *home*; and in order to settle this
question, we concluded to write to Sonoma coun-

ty and have our mail forwarded to Brown's Valley, and on the following Sunday morning we set out for Brown's Valley for our mail, also to see if we could find any encouragement offered us in opening a new account at some provision store. Brown's Valley was distant about seven miles, and our trail lay over a very rough, mountainous country. We were dressed in our best attire. Reed had on a pair of cow-skin shoes, but wore no socks; a slouched hat, turned down before and turned up behind, and a pair of pants, which, owing to frequent patching, no doubt bore a striking resemblance to a noted coat worn by Joseph of old:—they were made up of many colors, all surmounted by a garment that might have been called, vest, coat or shirt, and as easily been proven to be neither. I wore a brimless hat, no coat at all, a pair of 'run-down' boots, and an old pair of canvas "overalls," which had been "half-soled" with a flour sack—and it so happened that the manufacturer's brand was left so that it was no trouble for any one behind me, to read the following familiar inscription: "*XXX Warranted.*"

In going to Brown's Valley we had to cross Dry Creek by walking through a flume that spanned the creek. This flume was one thousand feet in length, and nearly one hundred feet above the level of the creek bed, and was used for conveying water for mining purposes from one hill-side to

another. Although a hazardous attempt for those
unaccustomed to such feats, we managed to cross
over in safety.   After getting our mail and finding the credit business abolished at the provision
stores, we set out on our return; a heavy rain set
in, and when we reached the Dry Creek flume,
we found the water rushing through it like a mill-
race, and with the storm roaring around us, our
only alternative was to crawl through that one
thousand feet of flume, on our hands and feet.
We reached our cabin shortly after dark, in a desperate frame of mind.

OUR PACK TRAIN IN THE OLD MINES.

It was then mid-winter, and Christmas morning found us frying the string our bacon had been
suspended with.   This we washed down with a
tin cup full of pepper-wood tea, and then we sat
down to reflect on the peculiarity of the situation.
All at once Reed started up and said he believed
there was a God in Israel yet, for the day before,
he had seen the tracks of a mountain hare in the
hills above us, and rising to his full length he

then and there declared that ere another sun went
down, he would have the meat of that hare, or
he would have *wool*.

I told him that I thought it would be useless
for him to attempt to get within reach of game
of any kind, as the sight of so oddly dressed and
as hungry a looking man as he was, would put
lightning speed into a snail. But Reed was determined, and went to a neighbor's cabin, borrowed
a gun—and sallied forth, while I went to our "out
door" camp-ground, built a fire under our big

camp kettle, and waited for coming events. I had
waited but a short time when a noise start-
led me. Stepping to an open place near the cabin, I was just in time to see a "jack-rabbit," with
its hair reversed, going like the wind through the
chaparral, and making tremendous leaps at ev-

ery turn in the trail, as it caught glimpses of its
desperate pursuer. Reed, having thrown away
his gun, was following the animal at a "break-
neck" pace. Seeing that it was a race *for life*, and
"no funeral of mine," 1 returned to replenish the
fire under the camp kettle.

About half an hour had elapsed, when the clat-
ter of worn out shoes, falling in rapid succession
on the stony ground, greeted my ears. I looked
only to see a continuation of the old race. This
time, the rabbit seemed to be making directly for
our cabin, but catching a glimpse of my half-soled pantaloons, he turned and made for the river;
and such wild leaps as that animal made, I have
never saw equaled—and Reed also made some
of the most inhuman jumps and plunges that a
mortal was ever guilty of, as, with scarcely anything on except an old pair of buckskin suspen-
ders (owing to frequent collisions with the chaparral), he dashed wildly in pursuit. The rabbit
leaped up a rocky point overlooking the river—
turned for an instant and gave one look at my
wild partner, who was coming down upon him
"Like a wolf on the fold"—and a moment later,
the terrified animal sprang into the roaring flood
and sank, to rise no more forever—that is, as a
matter of course, "hardly ever." It is unnecessary to add that game of all kinds speedily departed from the foot-hills in that vicinity.

REED'S POSITION AFTER THE RACE.

It was now evident that we would have to *move* or *starve*, and we very naturally decided upon the former course. Mr. Oliver Wescott (a son of the toll-bridge keeper) had a desire to work in the Redwoods of Sonoma County, and told us if we would aid him in securing a situation in that locality, he would furnish the money, and pay our way. As Reed and I were both very "promising" men, we promised Wescott to do our best for him, and the next morning we were on our way to our old haunts, where we arrived safe and tolerably sound. Reed found his old place vacant in the blacksmith shop at Sebastopol; and a few days afterward, Wescott and I started for the Redwood country on Russian river—distant about twelve miles.

We intended stopping for the night with an old friend of Reed's; he had a timber claim, and we hoped to secure a situation with him.

After walking about nine miles we entered
Pocket Canyon, and before proceeding far, mam-
moth trees surrounded us on every side, deeply
impressing us with their immensity; but I will
here add that I cannot accurately describe the
grandeur of a redwood forest. I once made the
attempt, but after a feeble effort, I was carried
home on a smoke-house door, and a n x i o u s
friends hung over me for "several times," fearful
lest I might recover, but when they found that
my personal property was mortgaged for its full
value, they soon nursed me up to my old wood
cutting weight. About noon we reached the old
woodman's cabin. It is unnecessary to give the
old man's name, for when I was a boy I was often "whaled" for "calling people names." The
old gentleman we found engaged in making shingles. Of course, we were invited in to dinner; the
old man was but an ordinary cook, yet I presume
he set out "the best in the shanty." Our dinner
consisted of cold hominy, cold potatoes, cold bacon, cold beans, and cold water—and as a natural consequence Wescott and I took a severe cold
before we got through.

After dinner, in company with the old man,
we started out on foot to explore the forest. It
was a clear day and just after noon, yet beneath
the shadows of the mighty forest, it was dark as
twilight in the Eastern States. Such trees I had

never dreamed of, and fancied that they existed only in the heated imagination of the writers of fiction.

Many Redwood trees on Russian river, I have good evidence to believe, stand fully 400 feet in height, and as many as ONE MILLION of excellent shingles have been made from the best portion of the trunk of a single tree; and as much as sixty thousand feet of clear lumber has been sawed from the trunk of one of these trees. We feel safe in saying that there is enough Redwood timber in the canyons adjacent to Russian river to fence in the world, build a city as large as London, and then have enough fire-wood left to supply all creation for several years.

The canyons of Russian river, near the coast, are thickly studded with Redwood trees, varying in size, from the tender sapling to giants measuring twenty-five feet in diameter. The bark on the larger trees varies from one inch to two feet in thickness; and it takes a good chopper from two to five days to fell one of these monsters.

This Redwood timber chops and splits very easy. I have seen plank, more than twenty feet in length, split or rived out with a common froe —in fact, nearly all the "weather-boarding" for the cabins of the woodmen in early days in this vicinity, was gotten out in this manner.

One remarkable feature of this Redwood timber is: it rarely or never decays. Trees, which to all appearance have lain on the ground for more than one hundred years, are as sound as ever.

Upon returning to the cabin, we talked the matter over, and finally formed a copartnernership—the old man to furnish the timber and the provisions, and Wescott and I to work with him, and take our pay in a portion of the timber we got out, consisting of shingles, pickets and shakes; and on the following morning we commenced operations in earnest.

The old man first put us to sawing up big logs of 'down timber,' with a nine-foot 'cross-cut' saw.

For a short time we will leave the subject of our present field of operations; but in another sketch, we will tell our readers something of our experience in the Redwoods—how we got out—and how we got back again.

'Twas a quiet Summer evening,
Just at the close of day,
When we came into the harbor
Of San Francisco Bay.

TO MY OLD ARMY COMRADES.

I come to you in friendship,
  From far distant Western lands,
Where the sun with golden brightness
  Shines on Pacific's sands;
Where old ocean's roar is heard,
  Whose billows wash the shore,
I come to you in friendship
  To review the scenes of yore.

While coming to this country
  Swiftly o'er the foaming tide
With nothing of this world to see,
  But billows far and wide,
When winds blew loud and furious,
  And storm-clouds gathered o'er,
I often thought of home and friends
  Upon a distant shore.

The memories of a comrade, dying,
  In my heart doth yet abide;
For they lowered him o'er the vessel,
  To sleep beneath the tide;
To sleep that last long sleep—
  With the blue waves overhead;
To sleep till Resurrection morn—
  'Till the Sea gives up its dead.

* * * *

I can ne'er forget that happy day,
  When we crowded 'round the "mate"—
And shouted, as he pointed out
  Pacific's "Golden Gate!"
'Twas a quiet Summer evening,
  Just at the close of day,
When we came into the harbor
  Of San Francisco Bay.

Since coming to this country,
  I believe what I've been told:
That men will risk their all on earth,
  For the shining stuff called gold;
They will brave the dangers of the deep,
  And toil in distant lands—
And never heed the steady fall
  Of Life's fast fleeting sands.

They will dig and delve in gravel—
  Through mud—through rain and cold,
And forget the God who made them,
  In their scramble after gold.
But perhaps, in other countries,
  Such men are not more rare
Than here in California—
  For we find them—everywhere!

    *   *   *   *

I remember yet, those by-gone days:
  The days of "Sixty-one,"
When Treason's clouds almost obscured
  The light of Freedom's sun;

When the drums beat up for volunteers,
  The coming storm to meet,
And we boys marched with steady tramp
  Down through the village street.

Those brave old days have vanished—
  And the "boys" are scattered, too;
In many Southern grave-yards sleep,
  The "Boys who wore the Blue."
And with these old-time memories,
  The longing comes anew—
To look once more upon the place
  My boyish foot-steps knew.

But the Sea is deep, and the way is long,
  And storms come oft, they say,
While Deserts lie on the "overland,"
  And dangers strew the way.
But some day, from my heart I hope,
  On my native soil to stand,
And see who's left of all the "boys,"
  In my dear old native land.

Though desert sands may intervene,
  With clouds on every breeze,
And though rude winds may whiten
  The waves on stormy seas—
Some day, I hope to wend my way
  Across the desert plain—
Or ride upon some gallant ship,
  High over the foaming main.

YUBA RIVER ONCE MORE.

OUR SECOND SEARCH FOR THE QUARTZ LEDGE.

AFTER putting in more than four months in the Redwoods, it suddenly became apparent to Wescott and I, that our ancient partner was determined to keep us continually at work on all the old 'down timber' that he could find on his claim. This was doubtless done for the purpose of

GETTING THE OLD MAN'S LAND CLEARED.

He would first have us sawing on a steep side-hill, then he would find an old blackened log in the canyon, and his next discovery would be

an old half-decayed stump in some almost inac-
cessible "gully;" and cheer us with the comforting remark: "Boys, when you get through with
that, I'll find something else for you." We con-
concluded to "get through" with it, and "find
something else" for ourselves—in short, we resolved to abandon the Redwoods, and make another effort to find the hidden quartz ledge on Yuba river. We had but very little cash on hand,
and could find no ready cash purchasers for our
share of the timber that we had worked up, and
we exchanged it for two 'mustangs' and an o l d
gold watch chain, supposed to be worth forty dollars, (although I since learned that some suppo-
sitions are decidedly erroneous); and then, with
about twenty dollars in cash, all told, we struck
out for the old mining region.

Although somewhat out of our direct route, we
concluded to go by the way of Ione Valley, Amador county, as Wescott had a relative living at
that place. As near as I can remember, this relative was a third cousin to a half-brother of Wescott's uncle—and as a natural consequence,—he
felt "*very near*" to my worthy partner.

Between Sacramento and Ione Valley we stopped at a wayside Inn; and in conversation with
the landlord, we found that he was tired of that
section of the country, and very anxious to seek
a new location; in order to do something for him

we refered him to either Sonoma or Marin county—telling him of the Redwoods of the former,
and of the beautiful Bay of Tomales, which in-
dents the borders of Marin. Seeing that the old
gentleman was struck (thunderstruck no doubt)
with our descriptive powers, we warmed up with
the subject, and launched off in an unabridged
description of Tomales Bay—its clam-beds, the
romantic Island—the shell beach and the splendid fishing—the matchless climate and charming scenery. At the conclusion of our remarks,
the old man—in a fearful state of excitement—
rushed to the barn, saddled his swiftest horse—
mounted him, and with jingling spurs,

HE WENT FLYING LIKE THE WIND,

in the direction of the famed country, l e a v i n g
orders for his wife to tear down and burn everything on the ranch, and follow him to the goodly
land.   We passed—(on up the road).

  During the following day we reached Ione Valley, and after a few days' rest, we resumed our
journey.

The dust was deep, the road growing more rugged as we neared the Sierra Nevada mountains. Passing through Placerville, we soon after crossed the South fork of American river. After crossing this river, our road extended for nearly two miles up a very steep grade. Higher and higher —up we went! We were getting into the Sierras. Here the scenery exceeds the loftiest imagination. A faint idea of its grandeur may be formed by imagining everything in the shape of d a s h i n g waterfalls, rushing torrents, springs of cold water gushing from a rocky ledge—narrow, winding trails along the mountain side, the crystal waters of a river far below, stately pines and firs, their tops reaching away up into the blue space overhead; while towering in majestic grandeur, snow-capped mountains glisten in the sun-light; while far back, stretching away, scattered in hazy, dream-like loveliness, the rustic homes of t h e ranchmen in the green valleys—the miner's cabin, and wigwam of the Indian—all flit before the eye in one circle-sweeping glance.

Such scenes are spread out in living reality all the year 'round beneath the skies of California. From Marysville, which is conceded to have the warmest temperature in central California, to any point fifty miles above, can be found as m a n y varying climates and changes of scenery, as the balance of the world can produce!

I still love the foot-hills of the Sierras, and the enchanting scenery that adorns their variegated steeps; and would never grow weary standing on their terraced heights, gazing upon the beautiful pictures there unfolded—painted and spread out by Nature's great artist, who dips his brush into unfading colors, and with one masterly stroke, produces a view that the brightest genius of nations strive in vain to imitate.

About 9 o'clock on the following morning we reached an old deserted town, bearing the name of Bottle Hill. The only inhabitant we discovered here was a Spanish woman; and she informed us that we were within a short distance of the middle fork of American river, at the same time pointing out a rude trail that led to the ferry by a much nearer way than the main road. This trail was seldom used except by pedestrians, as horsemen deemed it unsafe to ride down its terrifying steeps. As we were in quest of adventure, we decided to take the trail; and soon after, set out upon one of the most perilous journeys I ever undertook. Many a time since, I have started from my slumbers as visions of the middle fork of American river flitted through my d r e a m s. A more precipitous trail it would be difficult to imagine. We soon dismounted, uncoiled our lariats and 'strung out,' driving our mustangs before us. The mountain that we were descending

was mostly covered with scrubby timber, yet at
one time during the descent we came to an open
space, which afforded us an opportunity to survey our position. We were mid-way on the side
of a lofty mountain which seemed almost per-
pendicular, its top towering thousands of feet over us, while thousands of feet below, appeared an
awful chasm—walled up with bluish-white rock,
 through which rushed a mad tor-
rent, looking, from our position,
like a silver thread. That silvery.
looking thread was the m i d d l e
fork of American river! But its
thundering voice, from our stu-
pendous height, we c o u l d n o t
hear. Our trail to the river led
in a zig-zag course; and it took
nearly three hours of unceasing
travel for us to reach the stream,
after apparently standing directly over it. As we descended, the
roar of the water gradually broke
in upon our ears, and when we reached the river, the noise of its swift waters was almost deafening. The ferry-man took one horse and man
over at a time, running his boat with rope and
tackle. The trail on the opposite side of the river was equally as steep and more destitute of
trees, and at one place it ran out to a bare point,
the river appearing below—on both sides of us.

Here we stopped to regain breath, and to g a z e upon the wild scene, until we grew faint and dizzy; and then continued the ascent, scarcely daring to look back until we reached the summit.

Two days after this, we reached Condemned Bar; and after making a careful survey of the premises, selecting a suitable camping place, and negotiating an armistice with the Chinamen; and also discovering that our finances were on the wane, the day after our arrival, we concluded to go up in the hills and see if we could discover some old settler or distant relative w h o could be induced to "put up" a little "grub" on the strength of our developing the hidden quartz ledge. Fortunate conclusion!

The next day about noon, we called on a family by the name of Green. Of course, it required but a few minutes to convince them that I was decidedly *green* too; and I told them of a host of my relatives in Illinois who were fully as *green* as I was. We took dinner with the family; and upon our departure for camp, Mrs. Green (Heaven bless her liberal soul), filled up a big basket with choice edibles for our especial benefit— which, after considerable coaxing on her part— we took! On the following day, while we were "probing" different portions of the Bar, a gentleman, who I will call Dunbrown, came along. He was the owner of a big ranch, and carried a high head, filled with speculative ideas of bewildering magnitude. He informed us that he was an "old Californian, and well posted." What he *did know* might have filled a large book, yet I still think what he *did not know*, would have filled a larger and much more salable volume. In order to test the contents of Condemned Bar, we concluded to dig a deep ditch the full length of the bar (about 400 feet); and it was one of the rockiest bars that was ever "slung" together from big boulders and tough clay; and as the digging would naturally be hard, we deemed it policy to see if we could "let the job" to Dunbrown.

Cautiously we took him to one side (of the bar) and gave him a hint of the glittering treasure, supposed to be covered up—told him our plans, and if he wished to obtain an equal slice in the "bonanza," he could have it by simply digging that ditch. No other man on top of ground could have secured such a "lay-out" (he was completely *laid out*), and Dunbrown took the job!

For seven long days he swung the mattock, and for seven days Wescott and "yours truly" lay in the shade, and hurrahed for the 'old Californian,' and told him to hew his way into the 'bowels' of that bar; but no signs of gold quartz showed itsself—and the deeper the ditch went down, more trouble was encountered by the boulders rolling in from the sides of the ditch; and finally Dun-

brown became discouraged and fearing lest the
"fool-slayer" might come along and "bag" all
three of us, we concluded to change programme
—in short, all of a sudden I took a notion to
give up mining. We held a consultation, and it
was agreed that Wescott and I should go back to
Sonoma county and bring Jones up to Yuba
river—and solve the mystery, and in the meantime Dunbrown was to keep possession of the
Bar. We then saddled our mustangs, and took
an affectionate leave of Dunbrown, hoping that
we might never meet him again, unless we were
perfectly assured that he was sick and unarmed.
We afterwards learned that he departed for his
home as soon as we were well out of sight. He
was, no doubt, as glad to get rid of us as we were
to get away from him.

Reader it is a terrible thing to be disappointed
in some genuine expectation. You are no doubt,
aware of this—most people are. I have met with
but few individuals who have reached the meridian of life, whose feet have not slipped more
than once while ascending the hill of life's aspir-
ations. Few of the mighty host that strike out
expecting to realize big expectations ever reach
the summit, and the majority of those who have
been successful, became so, not so much by their
own exertions as by some freak of fortune or
luck, or through the assistance of friends.

I belong to the class whose feet are much given to "slipping," and for the benefit of those who never get beyond the "foot hills" of this life, I write this crude sketch. If any of my statements seem exagerated, I believe I can truly say, such things have happened. Life illustrated—as it was, is, or may be, produces a curious combination. Pictures of every-day life are seldom over-drawn. The gilded side is generally thrown to the public; it takes better; is more popular, you know. Anything that is popular always takes well in this age of gilded refinement, even though one-half the population is beggared by its application.

We concluded to return to Sonoma county by the way of Ione Valley, and during the afternoon of the second day after leaving the Bar, we accidently stumbled upon two small shocks of hay (the entire product of a mountain ranch). We purchased the whole crop, tied it to our saddles and proceeded on our journey. Several miles widened between us and the last inhabited house, when sundown found us on the banks of Deer Creek; and we proceeded to build our camp, to pass the loneliest night I ever experienced in the mountain wilds of the Far West.

A few deserted miners' cabins were scattered along the bank of the creek—relics of '49—old, dilapidated, and fast crumbling into decay, which served to increase our loneliness, as we peered through the open door-ways and wondered as to the fate of their former occupants.

Night came on, settling over us with the darkness of Egyptian gloom. No sound broke the silence save the waters of the creek, rippling over its rocky bed. Our horses were tied to trees near by, giving them about one-half of the hay, putting the remainder under our blankets, to serve as pillows for us that night and feed for our ponies in the morning: and then we lay down to sleep.

How long I slept I know not, but I do know that some time in the night I was awakened by a severe pinch from my companion. In a whisper, I enquired if he knew where *I* was, and also what was the matter with *him?* He replied that a strange feeling had taken possession of him, and *stillness* instead of *noise* had awakened him. The darkness seemed oppressive. Our horses were apparently sleeping in blissful ignorance of the terrible ague that shook their masters. Lighting a match I discovered that it was just midnight; and by the flickering glare of the match, I caught a glimpse of my companion's face; and I wish to say right here, that if I ever did have any doubt as to my companion being a *white* man, that one glance dispelled all doubt. Just then it occurred to both of us that "feeding time" had arrived— thus insuring an early start in the morning, and

we arose to give our horses the balance of the
hay—when judge of our surprise when we found
that *our hay was all gone!* lt had been taken out
from under our heads! *Hush!*

In amazement, on hands and knees, we crawl-
ed over what we supposed embraced a wide circle,
feeling for that hay, in which *feeling* operation
we got separated from each other—and then for
once, as soon as this fact was discovered, we sim-
ultaneously broke the stillness of the night, by
fairly shrieking: "Child, whar is you?" As we
were not over three feet apart at the time, it is
unnecessary to say, we soon got together. In
the morning a "tow-path" was plainly visible—
extending around, and very close to our sleeping
place, which we had "burrowed" out while making the "wide circuit" above referred to.

To this day, what became of the hay, is a mystery to me. Something, or somebody must have
strayed into our camp with noiseless tread—
"gobbled" our feed, and silently glided away.

We both lay awake during the remainder of
the night, scarcely daring to move. Every few
minutes, one of us would pinch the other—as if
to say: *"Did you hear anything?"* And as our
imagination became more heightened, the keen-
er became the pinches. For my part, I was almost pinched to death—and my companion—
poor fellow—he has been a confirmed cripple

ever since!—A mere wreck of his former s e l f.
The last account I had of him, he was roaming
through the Redwood forests on Russian r i v e r,
in search of light employment.

About three days after leaving our camp on
Deer Creek, we reached Ione Valley—two of the
"flattest broke" men California ever saw! And
the question, how to get back to Sonoma county
without money, was the leading problem that
puzzled our brains. There seemed but one alternative—*melt up that forty dollar watch chain and
sell the gold!* We accordingly placed the chain
into a ball of mud, heated it at a blacksmith's forge
until it was "red hot," and upon breaking the ball
open, we found a hand-full of metal pieces, bearing a strong resemblance to coarse, or "nugget"
gold—and then we formed our plans. Wescott
was to remain in Ione Valley and work a few
days for his *relative*, while I would try to make
my way to Sonoma county, on the strength of
the gold nuggets.

Sacramento was distant about 45 miles; and
about nine o'clock one morning, I mounted my
mustang and "clattered."

In some respects I might have been termed a
"singed cat"—that is, I was really worth more
than outward appearances indicated. I had *seventy cents in cash* (mostly silver), an old rusty revolver, a "bull's-eye" watch, a mustang (which

had been appraised at four dollars), and a melted
watch chain; and it is reasonable to suppose that
few strangers would have taken me for the possessor of the wealth I actually controlled.

At noon I stopped and got my horse fed, which
little act of foolishness cost me fifty cents. I had
twenty cents left! No doubt I presented the appearance of a *magnificent ruin*, as I rode into the
city of Sacramento about four o'clock in the afternoon. My coat was *invisible* to the naked eye,
but my toes were *visible*; my roll of blankets was
torn to shreds; my hat was merely a *rim*, while
my auburn locks waved to and fro, toying with
the summer breeze—and only twenty cents in
my pockets! I first put my mustang in a livery
stable and told the keeper that I might tarry in
the city for several days. After scrutinizing me
for a few moments, he informed me that "small-
pox was raging in Sacramento!" I told him that
I had *wintered on the Yuba*, and in my case, an
epidemic would be a relief. I then made my way
to the "Western House," gave my revolver to the
clerk, telling him to '*handle it very carefully*,' at
the same time informing him that in all proba-
bility I would recruit my secular system at the
dining table of the "Western" for the space of a
week. The clerk 'smole' a pensive smile, and said
he would put on an extra dray when the market
opened.

My next move was in the direction of an Assay office, which I soon found, and produced my nuggets. The assayer examined the pieces, testing them carefully, and then informed me that there was probably *three* dollars worth of gold in the whole lot—and it would cost just *four* dollars to assay it!

Was that me or some other waif of humanity standing on the street in the crowded city of Sacramento, after a ride of nearly fifty miles— with empty pockets, and my mustang in the livery stable—eating ten cents' worth of hay at every mouth-full, and taking fresh bites with alarming rapidity? I ran my hands into my pockets, and finding *just twenty cents,* I became thoroughly convinced that *it was me!*

A thousand thoughts hurried through my mind. Other men had stood on these same streets—all the way from the days of '49—and men were standing on the streets of Sacramento now—just as flat broke as I was; and then and there, I resolved to return to Sonoma county—though one hundred toll-bridges, spanning as many rushing torrents, lay between!

Knowing that the bridge over the Sacramento river would be closed at six o'clock, I hurried to the livery stable and told the keeper that I wished to give my mustang a bath in the river. He said he considered that an eminently proper thing to do; and he also intimated that a bath would greatly improve my appearance. I took the hint, and in order to get even with him, I postponed my return to that stable for an indef- inite period.

Time was flying, and I galloped to the hotel, and calling the clerk to one side, I told him that I had met a friend from the country, and t h a t friend insisted on my going out and spending the night with him. The clerk handed my revolver to me, patted me on the shoulder and to l d me to "go to the country by all means."

After leaving the hotel, I "scampered" for the bridge, where I arrived just in time, paid out my last cent for toll—crossed the river, and after go- ing about two miles, I stopped at a country tav- ern, where I registered myself as a second-rate busted miner, and put up for the night.

My mustang was provided with comfortable quarters, while I was assigned a place in the *dog shed*. The next morning I presented the hostess with one of my choicest "nuggets"—supposed to be worth more or less. Of course, I would n o t have done this with everyone (I could not afford it), but "seeing it was her," I must be liberal, for I had come a stranger—*and was taken in* (to the dog house).

Soon after I mounted my "plug" and contin- ued on my journey; and by being liberal in dos-

ing (bull-dosing) out my "nuggets" I reached
Barker Valley, where I fortunately fell in with a
gentleman named Cunningham, formerly of Peoria, Illinois. He was then traveling in the interest of one of the San Francisco Daily papers;
and after hearing a little of my mining experience, he held out a hand full of gold and silver,
and told me to take out all I needed to carry me
safely to my destination. I did so, and afterwards I had the pleasure of returning to him the
amount in full. When Mr. Cunningham tendered me the money, he told me, if in after years,
I ever met an unfortunate brother, and could do
so, to give to him even as he had given to me—
and that was all he asked of me in return. In
my journal of every-day life, I have written Mr.
Cunningham down as a *Christian of full stature.*

I reached Sebastopol in safety and found myself once more with friends, and at which place,
I remained until my partner, Wescott, arrived
from Ione Valley, and soon after, we went up to
our old haunts in the Redwoods, on Russian river, where Wescott took up a timber claim, and
went to shaving shingles and such other l i g h t
work as the severe pinching he had received on
Deer creek allowed him to do; and I took a job
of hauling shingles from the woods to Santa Rosa,
distant nearly twenty-five miles—with an ordinary farm wagon, and a single yoke of oxen.

The *first* trip I made, consumed the best part of five days. The load of shingles came to nine dollars; and the food for myself and oxen came to seven dollars and fifty cents. That's what I call doing business with an ox team.

The *second* trip I made with that span of oxen *hasn't come off yet!* My employer blamed me for being too long on the road, and I blamed the oxen. The case, as to who was right and who was wrong, remains undecided.

About this time, I received a letter from Reed, informing me that there was a vacancy in the blacksmith shop, and, as he knew I was unable to pound hot iron, I could get a situation just to stand at the bellows and do the *blowing.* That suited me; therefore I settled up with my employer (I was only owing him eighty cents), and set out on foot for Sebastopol, where I was received by my old companion, with open arms.

OUR REDWOOD CABIN.

How brightly it gleams: that home in the forest,
  As old recollections float up from the past;
The tall forest trees standing thickly all 'round it,
  With their shadows so pleasant that were over us cast;
The canyon below, and the brook that wound through it,
  Whose clear waters served us in place of a well;
And close by the stream, to the right, as you'd view it,
  Was our cabin of Redwood that stood in the dell.

The old wagon road winding through the deep valley—
  The young evergreens, springing up by the way,
Have left in my heart a lasting impression,
  That shines from the past like a bright Summer day;
And the bridge made of bark, and the old tree so near it,
  Up-rooted by storms—lying just as it fell:
Yet dearer than all—I shall ever revere it—
  Is the old Redwood cabin that stood in the dell.

The soft sighing winds, and the roar of old ocean,
  Sang us melodies rare, through the still hours of night,
And their memories oft fill my heart with emotion,
  Though that home in the forest has faded from sight.

Of all earthly spots, that one seems the fairest:
Like a drink of cold water from a deep crystal well,
Or like an oasis on Life's dreary desert—
Was the cabin we built in the cool shady dell.

*   *   *   *   *

Though years have gone by, and that home is far distant,
And between us the sands of the desert now swell,
Yet mem'ry grows bright as it beckons me Westward,
To that old cabin home that stood in the dell.
The rudely built cabin—the "shake" covered cabin,
Our cabin of Redwood that stood in the dell.

Mason City, Illinois, 1870.]

RUSSIAN RIVER VALLEY, AND THE BIG CAMP MEETING.

AUTUMN in 1865 found me in the blacksmith shop at Sebastopol—but Reed and I were getting *too tired to be useful;* and learning that an o l d fashioned Camp Meeting was soon to be held in the neighborhood of Healdsburg, on Russian river, we resolved to go.

I remember well the morning we started. We had managed to borrow a small bay horse and a rude cart, or "dug-out," from our employer, and mounted on a spring seat that Reed had attached to our odd looking craft, we extended a Commanche Indian-like invitation to the small boys on the street to "clear the road"—and we meandered, feeling sure that we had left a vacancy in the sleepy old town of Sebastopol that would not be satisfactorily filled until our return.

Our road lay through Green Valley, a beautiful little vale, skirted with tasty vineyards a n d thrifty orchards. As my companion wished to transact some business for his employer, with a party who resided in the Redwoods, we took this round-about way. We arrived in the afternoon at the home of the party who Reed wished to see, and here we were prevailed upon to remain over night; and on the following morning we "geared up" that small "red horse" and started for Healdsburg—the Camp Meeting, and all way stations.

Our route now lay directly up R u s s i a n River Valley—one of the loveliest regions that lies beneath the skies of this sunny land. On our winding way, we crossed Russian river n i n e times—and other streams in proportion.

On every hand, from one end of this valley to the other, the scenery is simply enchanting in its picturesque beauty. Flourishing corn fields—immense stacks of Wheat, Oats and Barley; orchards groaning under their tempting burdens of delicious fruit—and rustic farm houses scattered up and down the valley, or dotting the hill-sides, all served to make up the picture of rural loveliness that charmed our eyes and thrilled o u r hearts with delight as we journeyed on the way.

The entire Russian River Valley, which may properly be considered as extending from Petaluma to Cloverdale—a distance of fifty miles—

all things considered, in my humble opinion, has no equal on the Pacific coast. The climate is mild and healthful. Water is plenty and of an excellent quality. No irrigation is required. Wheat in favorable seasons and in favored localities, has yielded as much as sixty bushels to the acre. Apples, Peaches, Pears, Plums, Apricots, Figs, and Grapes, yield enormous crops; and vegetables of almost every variety are successfully grown.

Cultivated land in this region (at this writing, 1885), ranges all the way from forty to s i x hundred dollars per acre—according to location, quality, and improvements.

About noon we arrived at Healdsburg, which we found to be a handsomely shaded village of perhaps five hundred inhabitants (This, the reader will please remember, was in 1865).

We drove straight to a Livery stable and Reed hailed the hostler "thusly;"

"I say, Mister, is there a tavering in this burg where a feller can git a squar meal at low rates?"

"Yez zur" said he, "that two-story frame right over thar, is a *staving house, you bet.*"

That was all we wished to know, and after telling him to shovel the shelled oats in alopathic doses into that red complexioned nag of ours, we made a wild dash for the hotel, and were s o o n engaged in getting away with a "square meal;" that is as much as to say: we consumed everything within a square yard of our immediate vicinity.

After a half-hour's violent wrestle with 'grub' at the dinner table, we took a stroll through the village, and admired much that we observed, but during our rambles, we experienced the sorrow of being unwilling spectators to a rough and tumble fight between two women (near neighbors), during which contest, snuff colored hair and crinoline sustained severe loss. We paused only long enough to shout: "Fight on, fair flowers of this sunny land; Northern chivalry behold and deplore your deeds." We understand that the battle continued until a female passer-by informed the belligerents that *calico had riz*, and that ended the fight!

In our further perambulations, we met an old acquaintance named Tom Clevinger. He was (as he expressed it), "one of the uncurried colts of New Jersey—storm tossed, weather-beaten and flat broke, but full of hope and "old Nick," combined."

Tom informed us that he had recently come to Healdsburg in search of employment, and for the past few days he had been working on probation in a blacksmith shop; and as the proprietor was a zealous Methodist, Tom had made up his mind to attend the Camp Meeting, in order to create a favorable impression on the mind of his employer; therefore we three concluded to go together; and after settling our hotel and stable bills, we *boarded* our little land schooner (that is, we placed a *board* across the rear end of the cart for Tom to ride on), flourished our seven foot pepperwood "gad" and "lit out."

Although the camp ground was just about one mile distant, by frequent inquiries along the road, we managed to reach the place before sundown.

We found a vast crowd assembled, with a goodly number of Ministers from various portions of the State. And among the other good things, we stumbled upon was, *a Free Dining Table! Hush! Be still. Be remarkably quiet.* Everything promised a good old-fashioned time; and we rejoiced that *we* were there, and also exceedingly glad to know that it was *us*.

The evening was beautiful—the occasion impressive. The surroundings exerted a soothing influence; and when the exhilerating aroma of smoking viands floated by us from *the free boarding tent*, visions of the far-away Yuba passed before my eyes; hungry memories stirred my soul, and with enthusiastic ecstasy, I grasped Reed by his right "bread hook," and shouted: "My old comrade, you and I together, to the hungry and brittle thread of hope, too oft have clung. Too often we have left the onion beds of reality, only

to clutch the bitter fruits of Sodom.   The r i c h
quartz ledge on Yuba river lies buried beneath
the reach of our resources. We have *hunted gold*
and *gathered dross.*   But here, on the generous
banks of this beautiful river, we have found
pasture; and so long as the tin trumpet's "toot"
calls us with due regularity to the free boarding
tent, let us abide." And Reed lifted up his lute-
like voice (which strongly reminded me of t h e
boom of a bittern), and said: "It is well,"—a n d
we tarried.

On the evening of our arrival we attended the
meeting, taking a position close to the preachers'
stand—and were very favorably impressed. After the services were over, finding no indications
of a cold lunch being passed around, we adjourned to a straw-stack and slumbered until the tin
horn sounded the cheering notes, which seemed
to say:

"Ye hungry, starving souls, draw near."

And then, without taking time to wash, comb,
or even shake the barley "beards" off our clothes,
we rushed at a 2:40 pace for the table, which we
reached about two lengths in advance of the fleet-
est Indian in the camp.

The majority of the boarders *dined*, but Reed,
Tom and your humble servant, considering ourselves somewhat *human*, contented ourselves by
simply *chawing* provisions and *pouring down* hot

coffee for about seventy minutes—and then, Tom told the folks to "bring on their preachers."

About ten o'clock in the morning we took our seats in the assembly, and listened to the Gospel's solemn warning.

It was Sunday. We were strangers in a strange land—far from the haunts of our nativity. Old memories were busy in our hearts; and that Sunday I shall long remember. The dark evergreen trees overhead—the wild birds flitting through the foliage, singing their sweet songs—all served to bring back to me, with all their freshness, the sweet pictures of childhood.

Hundreds of people in the vast crowd, h a d come from the mountains and distant valleys— twenty—fifty, and even one hundred miles away! Quite a number of the Red children of the West had also gathered on the outskirts of the camp, gazing steadily on the "pale-faced" minister— listening with wrapt attention as the speaker, in thrilling tones, exhorted the wanderers of every nation to come home to God.

My heart was deeply touched; and I felt that I had wandered a long way from my Father's house. At the close of the sermon, the most intense feeling prevailed. All present seemed to realize that *God was there.*

Old woodmen and miners—many of t h e m wrecks on the mad sea of Life, stood up and testified to that brighter hope—*Faith in Jesus!*

Old soldiers and sailors, bronzed by wearing service on land and sea—men who had trod the streets of old Jerusalem, and had mocked a n d blasphemed in the sacred places in the City of David, on that quiet Sunday morning, rose up, and with tears coursing down their cheeks, prayed that they might yet be permitted to moor their storm-tossed barks on *the Golden shore.*

But time sped by, and the big Camp Meeting on Russian River came to a close; yet, even now, a beautiful vision gleams in the distance, l i k e *"Apples of Gold in Pictures of Silver."* And the beautiful valley—the rippling River, and the old Camp-ground, I still see, through the fast fading portals of the *far back,* as old recollections sweep as it were, the "silver chords" of memory, with an angel's hand.

Twenty years have gone by since we "Tented on the old Camp-ground." Healdsburg has grown to be a flourishing city of nearly five thousand inhabitants. The "Iron Horse" snorts in the valley, and drives the swift wheels of progress from salt water to the mountains, consigning to oblivion the old traveled ruts of former years; and t h e hum of a riper civilization follows in their wake, and catching up the echo from the hill-sides— rolls in gladsome tones through the beautiful valley—down to the Sea.

LINES TO OLIVER WESCOTT.

The following poem of suspicious measure, is one of my first attempts at rhyming; and may be considered an "off-hand" invitation to my Yuba river companion of 1865, to induce him to return with me to the "States." After reading this poem, it is unnecessary to state that Wescott remained in California.

Old friend, let's go where fragrant blossoms
    Load the air with sweet perfume ;
Where, for such men as you and I,
    There's always "lots" of room ;
Where the fruit defies for flavor,
    All the lands 'long side the Sea—
Say, don't you feel like starting—
    To that happy land with me ?

Where the blue birds and the black birds and the jay birds
        sing so merrily,
    In the early dewy morn—
Making music for the plow-men,
    In the fields of yellow corn and white corn, sugar corn and
        seed corn and other varieties of corn.
Where people can be happy,
    If they only try to be ;
Then sell your claim for whatever you can get,
    And sling yourself back home, and settle down close to me.

Where wild grapes do hang in clusters,
  Throughout the forests brown,
And black haws and red haws and persimons and pawpaws,
      like a lot of us boys at the close of a dance one night,
  Lie scattered on the ground.
To that land that lies so far away—
  On Mississippi's shore,
Where oft you've battled with the tide, while working on the
      railroad for ten dollars a week—
  In those good old days of yore.

Dear friend, my heart grows sad—
  I can scarce suppress a sigh,
To think that as well a put up man as you are, would come
      away out here to chop wood and maul rails and shave
      shingles, and then curl his self up—
  And then pile down—and then die;
For there's nothing on this dreary coast
  But sighs and endless fears,
That follow us, like a well trained coon dog, from early in the
      morning until about two hours after dark—
  Adown the steep of years.

ADIEU TO CALIFORNIA.

[Written on the Steamer "Golden City," on my return to Illinois, by water, in 1866].

I'm going home—O, California—
  Fades thy land-scape from my view;
Through the Golden Gate we're passing,
  Out upon the ocean blue.
All thy mountains, hills and valleys
  Look to me more lovely, now;
All thy fields and shady wood-lands,
  With fresher verdure seem to glow.

Oft while in your lonely gulches,
  Seeking for the golden sand,
I have cursed the luck of miners,
  And Pacific's sunny strand;
But when thoughts come crowding o'er me,
  Of my leaving thee for aye,
Forgotten are all disappointments—
  I can but say: a kind adieu.

Far behind me now are fading
The checkered scenes of Western life ;
No more will I come back to view them,
Filled as they were with toil and strife.
The White sails in the wind are flut'ring ;
My eyes once more rest on the land ;
But fast 'tis fading—fast receding ;
Again I wave the friendly hand.

*　　*　　*　　*　　*

Around our ship the shadows gather,
Bright, o'er the waves, the moon-light beams,
While far above our noble bark,
The faithful head-light gleams ;
The sunny land far out has faded,
Old ocean's waves around me swell ;
Home voices in my heart are whispering :
Pacific shores—a long farewell.

WE "ABOUT FACE," AND STEAM FOR ILLINOIS!

Owing to my old journal being burned some five years ago, I am somewhat at fault in regard to dates; yet as near as I can remember, I made my arrangements to return to Illinois about the tenth of April, 1866. Jenkins, of Illinois, and Reed, my first companion in the search for the hidden quartz ledge, and the Author, concluded that we would "all go home together." We used our strongest arguments to induce Wescott to accompany us, but he had fallen in love with a pretty girl in the Redwoods, and avowed his intention to *stay with her*; and a few days before our departure, we sent an invitation to him to come and see us and bid us good-bye. Two days after the invitation was sent, Wescott answered in person; and when the morning of April tenth came around, we indulged in a general leave-taking; and I take pleasure in saying that when I bid good-bye to Oliver Wescott, I shook the hand of an honest man and a true friend.

Arriving in San Francisco, we secured tickets for New York, via. Panama and Aspinwall, taking passage to Panama on the steamer *Golden City*, and from Aspinwall to New York on the steamer, *Costa Rica*. Of course, we took the *steerage*. Had there been a *second-grade steerage*, we would have taken that; and to be honest about this business, in our dilapidated financial condition, we would have *taken anything except Castor oil*. The journey to New York was a very pleasant one, and as near as I can remember, consumed about twenty-two days. We were nearing *home!*

At New York I doffed my old California "working harness," bought a ticket to Peoria, Illinois, and by careful count, found that I had *just Five Dollars left!*

Kind Reader, after an absence of more t h a n *two years*, fraught with toil, hardship, deprivations and disappointments, I was returning to my old *home* with *empty pockets!*

In due course of time I arrived at Peoria, and then went down the Peoria, Pekin and Jacksonville Railroad to Forest City station, distant from Mason City about sixteen miles.

At this point I stopped for a few hours to rest, and to inquire of the citizens if they had any definite idea as to who I was and where I was going. During the afternoon I met a teamster going to Mason City, and with him I made a bargain to convey me to my home for the insignificant sum of two dollars! I arrived at *home* about dark, with *exactly one dollar and fifty cents in my pockets!*

For the first month after my arrival home, I was kept pretty busy answering questions a n d rehearsing my experience about life and times in California. With the men, I succeeded v e r y well. With my young lady friends, the case was more difficult; for they all seemed anxious to see some specimens of *genuine California gold*, that all returned Californians were supposed to possess.

For the inspection of the more inexperienced, I produced the few remaining relics of *that melt-ed watch chain!* That satisfied them. Another portion of my fair interviewers I silenced by say-ing: "Ladies, you are aware that at the present time, *gold* is very *high*; and as a business man, with an eye to business, I exchanged all my gold for *greenbacks!* By this innocent strategy I saved my credit. But I could not remain idle and do anything like a "land office business in Illinois.

I had no money, but found *friends* who were willing to aid me, and they asked me: What do you wish to do? Having read one of "Josh Billings' health Almanax," and knowing the po-tency of a box of compound cathartic pills, prop-erly handled, I answered:

I want to be a Druggist,
  And with the "druggers" stand;
With powerful mixtures on my shelves,
  And a pill-box in my hand.

That settled the entire business, and in much less time than it takes to change postmasters, I was duly installed in my new position, surrounded by four caddies of fine-cut chewing tobacco, a lot of cigars, a keg of whiskey (for *medicinal purposes*), twenty pounds of quinine, half a barrel of seidlitz powders, a jar of rhubarb, sixteen gross of Bateman's drops, and *three crates of Harlem oil.* (This last item done the business for your beloved writer).

There was a great deal of ague in Central Illinois nineteen years ago, and it did not take me long to discover the fact that quinine and whiskey were generally prescribed as the great specific for all diseases of a malarial character; and as a natural consequence, Harlem oil was laid in the shade; for it did appear as if almost every body was either shaking with the ague, or had symptoms that called for the standard remedy. Often, as a healthy patient came in, I soliloquized "thusly:,' This man does not appear to be very sick, although he says he is *all doubled up*, and if his prescription is not filled, he might get most awful sick, and then blame the druggist—and a druggist cannot see his fellow-man suffer when the remedy is at hand. I grew tired of the drug business. There was too much ague there, and no disease so far as I could learn that could be reached, either by Harlem oil or Bateman's drops, and I began to inquire for the man who wished to invest in a small but carefully selected stock of drugs. I found my man. He offered me one

hundred and fifty dollars for the entire stock—
and fifty dollars more if I would keep the Harlem
oil!   I closed the trade on the first proposition.

In the meantime, it may be news to the general reader to learn that old father Time h a d
kept his mill running right along; and the first
thing I knew, the Summer of 1867 was in the
field—and found me out of business.

At this time Mason City was a town of about
three hundred inhabitants, with no railroad facilities; yet among its population it contained a
printer: Elder J. M. Haughey, who preached to
the apostate sons of Adam on Sundays, and op-
erated a job printing office during week days; he
had about a hat-full of second hand type and an
old press that was made by a man named Jones.
It was the oddest looking press my eyes ever had
the chance to rest upon.   There were 'no *flies* on it.'
It had an inking cylinder about the size of a nail
keg located at the rear end, and this cylinder's
business (when the press was in motion), was to
execute a sort of double summersault, glide under the press and then come to a dead halt, in order to give the office "devil" time to take a fresh
chew of tobacco, and then it would slowly mean-
der to its first position and await further orders.
This press (I have been informed), was capable
of making several impressions every now a n d
then.   At last accounts it was in the field—but

Jones, the inventor—he died of remorse y e a r s ago! I am sorry for Jones.

To make a long story short; after thoroughly canvassing the field, Mr. Haughey and myself concluded to establish a newspaper. Our means were limited, but enterprising citizens put their hands into their pockets and told us to bring on the necessary machinery and *fire up*.

We then purchased an outfit from Rounds & James' type foundry, of Chicago, hired a printer, and on the Fourth day of July, 1867, the firm of Haughey & Walker issued the first copy of the Mason City Weekly *News*. (At this writing, the old paper still waves, with Haughey at the helm, although its name has been changed to that of *Independent*).

Our paper created a boom in the little t o w n . Subscribers came to the office in crowds; many of the business men subscribed by the year for ten, fifteen and twenty copies each, and also advertised beyond our expectations, so much so as to make it necessary to enlarge our sheet twice during the first year. Money *rolled* into our office, and we soon forgot the bitter experience of former years. A branch of the Chicago, Alton and St. Louis Railroad was built through Mason City, to be followed a few years later by the Indianapolis Bloomington and Western Railroad.— Real estate loomed up. Two handsome public school buildings were erected at a cost of nearly forty thousand dollars. Churches, banks, an opera house, and all conveniences and essentials of an enterprising town were soon represented; and Mason City became widely known as the m o s t wide-awake and flourishing town in central Illinois; and to-day it boasts a population of nearly five thousand people.   The low lands in the county have been thoroughly ditched and drained, greatly improving the sanitary condition— driving malarial diseases from its borders—causing the once dreaded name of *ague* to sound like a wail from the past. *Vive la Mason City.*

MY FIRST NEW YEAR'S GREETING.

To the Patrons of the Mason City "NEWS."

January First, 1868.

We come to you: our patrons,
  With love on every hand,
To scatter joy and gladness
  Throughout this happy land!
The old year that has passed away,
  To some, a life-time seems:
For with it faded swiftly by—
  A throng of happy dreams.

And some with joy, look back,
  To the days of '67,
Whose every hour seemed wafting them
  A little nearer Heaven.
Bright youth grew up, with rosy cheek;
  Old age lay down to die—
But *Time*, ne'er heeding, marched along,
  As the old year glided by.

We've a sigh for those who sorrow,
  And a smile for the blithe and gay,

And we come with love to greet you,
  On this jolly New Year's day.
While the golden rays of Summer,
  Shone o'er the fields of grain,
We launched our little paper,
  In this city on the plain.

And now, though fierce winds whistle,
  O'er all this land sublime,
We'll try and make it to you all,
  Seem just like Summer time.
To the great lakes of the Northland,
  To Mountain, Hill and Plain,
To the Cities and the Hamlets,
  And to old Ocean's main,—

We come to you with greeting,
  That we hope will always last,
To bind the sunny present,
  With the shadows of the past;
That your pathway to the future,
  Though a cloud may o'er it be,
May lead you safely where you can
  A "silver lining" see.

We greet our beloved patrons,
  From Sitka to the Rio Grande;
From the hills of the Old Dominion,
  To Pacific's golden strand,
And we are proud to tell our readers,
  That the Old Flag, yet unfurled,
Still floats high o'er America,
  At peace with all the world.

Every Island of the ocean,
And the Nations from afar,
Look on our glorious Ensign,
As the bright and morning star;
All countries do us honor,
And award the highest palm,
To the LIGHT-HOUSE OF CREATION,
Our dear old "UNCLE SAM!"

And the time is fast approaching,
(As we think God wills it should,)
When this mighty Universe will be
One common brotherhood.
The cable spans the Ocean,
And the Railroad's going through,
Which like a mighty chain will bind
The Old world with the New.

And we hope our new acquaintance,
So recently begun—
Will only end with us on earth,
When *all our work is done.*
And now, while pleasant memories
Of old times are hovering near—
We wish our friends, all o'er the land—
A Happy—Glad, New Year.

BACK TO CALIFORNIA.

I TRY THE OVERLAND.

I continued in the newspaper business u n t i l the Spring of 1874—nearly seven years—and it found me completely broken down in h e a l t h . My physicians advised me to try a change of climate; and strange as it may appear, I resolved to *return to California!*

In the meantime, I had married, and a family was growing up around me at a rate that would have been positively alarming, had the aforesaid calamity overtaken me years before on the banks of Yuba river. We decided to leave Illinois, and accordingly, I sold out—home, business and everything else in the shape of property: and now, if the Reader will bear with me, I will endeavor to give the main outlines connected with a journey from Illinois to California—on an *emigrant train.*

The 17th day of June, 1874, was the day of our departure from Mason City—going from there to Bloomington, where we boarded the Chicago, Rock-Island & Pacific train, for Omaha, by way of Peoria. Our route from Bloomington to Omaha, led us through as lovely a region as the sun shines on, for surely, there are few fairer regions on this green earth, than that portion of country traversed by the Chicago, Rock-Island & Pacific Railroad—through Illinois and Iowa—in the month of June. Matchless pictures of Nature's landscape painting, greet the eye, in one continuous panorama—on every hand—for hundreds of miles.

Omaha (which we reached in due season), we found to be a bustling city of more than thirty thousand population. It is the starting point for travelers bound for the Far West; and at the big Union Depot (which is now located on the Iowa shore, at Council Bluffs), getting on board a Western-bound emigrant train, with a family of small children, with the accompanying, indispensible camp equippage—blankets, pillows, cooking utensils, provisions, etc., is no small job. There is always a large crowd, of cosmopolitan make-up—a general rush—a terrible jam, and dire confusion. There is the usual quota of swearing, hundreds of crying children, a small regiment of pettish women—a host of surly men—innumerable pick-pockets and loafers—the unpleasant situation being relieved, only by the happy thought, that perchance there might be one or two honest printers in the crowd.

At Omaha, the emigrant from the farther East becomes aware of the fact that a change will soon "come over the spirit of his dreams;" for at this point the *gold* and *dross* of humanity are separated. The *sheep* and the *goats* are divided—the *goats* as a natural consequence, take the first-class trains, and the *"sheepish"* looking emigrant is given a stiff piece of pasteboard, setting forth the fact that the holder thereof is an *emigrant* of the *first water*, and must retain his or her seat for at least *nine consecutive days,* if aforesaid ticket-holder hopes to reach the *Golden Shore*, as "stop-over" checks are not on this programme. F i r s t class passengers only, are allowed these luxuries; and this accursed policy of "man's inhumanity to man" has made "countless thousands mourn."

After getting our trunks weighed, and, as usual, paying for a difference in weight in favor of the U. P. road (for baggage gains largely in traveling through Illinois and Iowa), we were next encountered by the Railroad Company's *"rope fiend,"* who sauntered up to us, and in a neighborly way, said: "By the way, Mister, I don't believe those trunks of yours are sufficiently strapped to stand the racket, clear through to California—but for twenty-five cents apiece, I will rope 'em up so *nothin'* can't shake 'em." We paid the sum demanded, and then stood by and saw this same railroad fiend *rope in* at least fifty other ignorant passengers. *This is one of the many little Railroad games*, which should receive the hearty condemnation of all classes of this Republic.

We got safely on board and secured our seats; and a few minutes later, I was thoroughly convinced that lumber and calico were certainly on the rise; for a man came into the car with t w o pine boards and a couple of old calico sacks, filled with saw-dust—and this man told us those articles were *just the thing* to fix up the hard seats, and convert them into comfortable s l e e p i n g berths. This was another *Railroad trick*. This "good Samaritan" told me that the usual price for such things in Omaha, was *five dollars*, but, (he added, confidentially), "As you were late in getting on board, you can have the whole out-fit *for two dollars and fifty cents!*" I looked at the hard seats, and then at my tired family, and— I closed the bargain right then and there; a n d after embracing my *benefactor*, and urging him to allow me to go out and order a cup of warm tea for him—in remembrance of h i s *Christian qualifications*, I bade him farewell—and hope to *never hear of him again.*

About five o'clock in the afternoon, the b e l l
rang—the engineer blew his whistle—and off we
started, at a speed that bore a strong resemblance
to the gait of a printer's "devil," when going on
an errand; and in somewhat less time than it
usually takes to get a claim through the United
States Pension Department, Omaha was fading in
in the distance—and the boundless region of
"*wind-loved*" Nebraska, was soon stretching out
on either side—and away beyond!

"Over the plains, so wide, so great,
　Like a snow-bound inland sea,
We whirled along from State to State,
Day by day, early and late,
　Towards the Western Sea.

And day and night, and night and day,
　With still, unceasing roar,
We glided by river and dale and hill,
O'er alkali plain and mountain rill,
　To the distant Sunset Shore."

The country, for two hundred miles West of
Omaha, in regard to natural beauty and fertility
of soil, is unequaled, and certainly offers rare inducements to people in search of cheap homes, in
a new and rapidly rising State.

We passed the towns of Fremont, Columbus,
Grand Island, North Platte and Sidney, and other places of minor importance—and all of them
appeared to be in a prosperous condition; and I
take pleasure in saying that so far, I have never

seen a town in the State of Nebraska, with a population of five hundred people, that did not have a good, substantial and commodious *School house.* It does not take lobbying and electioneering to build School-houses in Nebraska. As a general rule, in that State, when the people wish to make a town, they build a good School house—and the town grows up around it.

On the third day after leaving Omaha, t h e entire State of Nebraska lay behind us, and the soil of festive Wyoming was pressed beneath us.

While traveling, with snail-like pace over this region, our eyes feasted upon the unsophisticated cactus, scattering antelope, prairie dogs, s t r a y buffalo, poor country, etc., until the grim peaks of the Rocky Mountains, loomed up in the distance; some were dark and frowning, some covered with verdure, and others mantled with snow.

The next point of interest was Cheyenne, 516 miles West of Omaha. Cheyenne has an elevation of 6,000 feet above Sea level. At this point we stopped for one hour, which time was principally occupied by the passengers in l a y i n g in a new supply of provisions, of which we found plenty, and at reasonable prices.

On the same evening after leaving Cheyenne, we reached Sherman (the summit). The elevation at this point is marked at 8,242 feet It is distant from Omaha, 550 miles.

Sherman is the highest point on this road, yet the ascent is so gradual that one can scarcely realize the immense height attained. The scenery is grand and beautiful, but tame when compared with the rugged steeps and dizzy precipices of the Wasatch and the Sierras.

In the due course of time we reached Ogden, where we changed cars, and were soon bowling along over the Central Pacific Railroad, at a rate of speed that seemed to say: "We'll get there by and by." After leaving Ogden, we traveled for several miles in plain view of Great Salt Lake, but the city of Salt Lake cannot be seen from the line of the Central Pacific.

Our time from Ogden until we reached California, was employed as usual, in buying grub, spanking the children, and looking out of the car windows, gazing (for the most part), upon what seemed to me, the most barren, and apparently God-forsaken country, that was ever manufactured from an inferior quality of gravel, sage-brush, sand and alkali. Just think of it! A little more than two t h o u s a n d miles from O m a h a to San Francisco, and fully twelve hundred of those miles pass through a country that is just about as devoid of vegetation as the bottom of an Illinois frog pond, at the close of a long, dry season! It struck me as the picture of desolation, clothed, not with *sack-cloth and ashes*, but *sand and alkali*.

We arrived in San Francisco on the ninth day after leaving Omaha; and I will also add, that I think the sights to be seen, and the lessons that may be learned along the road, will amply repay any one for making the journey from the East to California.

I could write a large volume, relating to t h e wonders and beauties of the Wasatch and Sierra Nevada mountains—if I only *had time*, and *knew how to do it.* In some places, while p a s s i n g through Weber and Echo canyons, t h e motion, jar, and rumble of the train, shook pebbles and dirt from the beetling crags, that hang over the road, and they came rattling down upon the tops of the cars and against the windows like h a i l - stones; while huge boulders, of many tons weight, hang in menacing attitude, hundreds of feet overhead, apparently ready to dash down and hurl the passing train into unfathomable chasms of inextricable and unregenerate absquatulation.— (The winding up of the above sentence is partly *o*-riginal, and partly *ab*-original). It was and is yet my opinion that on some quiet evening, somebody or somebody else, will get hurt on the Central Pacific railroad.

To people in moderate circumstances, and who have a desire to come to California, we w o u l d say: If you do not value time too highly, and are not ashamed to ride in company with *respectable*

p e o p l e—*take an Emigrant train.* If, at a n y
time, you get tired riding, you can get down and
walk, and employ your leisure time in gathering
the docile cactus, or curious pebbles, and resume
your seat at pleasure. (We say this with all due
deference to the speed of the average emigrant
train).

To the emigrant, starting out on the Overland,
we would say: If you don't do anything else that
is worthy of note, by all means, lay in a heavy
stock of provisions, for you will need all you can
carry; and it would be good policy to continue
"laying in" grub at every station along the road,
where an opportunity presents itself, for it is truly wonderful, the amount of provisions a small
family will consume on a two thousand m i l e s
journey—on a slow train.

In laying in your outfit, do not put too much
confidence in dried beef; it is not the thing for
travelers over a desert country, as it requires entirely too much *irrigation.* Corned beef and ham
thoroughly cooked and well freshened, will answer; and with coffee and tea, crackers, and fresh
bread, (which you can buy along the road), and
with plenty of jellies for the children, will bring
you through in good shape. Do not be so reckless
as to invest in dried buffalo meat, that is often
found at the stations, unless you want to *shingle
your house with it*—after you get through; for you
can never chew it with those teeth of yours!

While in San Francisco, among the many places of interest, we visited Woodward's Gardens,
which at that time, was, for all classes, the most
popular resort in the city. The inclosure embra-
ces about six acres. The entrance is through an
architectural gateway, surmounted by four colos-
sal statues, or carved figures. We first made our
way to the Museum, the doorway to this institution being formed by the jaw-bone of a *bird* called the *whale*, the two lower ends resting on t h e
stone foundation, and coming together at the top
at the height of eighteen feet, formed a perfect
oval arch. In the museum we found almost everything that we had ever seen or heard of: min-
eral specimens from California, Australia, Arizona, Mexico, Nevada, Colorado, Montana and Ida-
ho; thousands of rare and beautiful shells of ocean,
curious old coins, bearing date long before t h e
time of the Cæsars; relics from Egypt and Pales-
tine; a piece of the great Chinese wall; old scraps
of history on parchment, centuries old; rusty ar-
mor that once gleamed on the crusaders in t h e
days of chivalry; the stump of the cocoa tree under which Capt. Cook was murdered by the Ha-
waiian savages—and a thousand other curiosit-
ies that space forbids mentioning. We then took
in the grand menagerie, the conservatory, zoo-
logical department, the shady dells,the aquarium,
the moving panorama of the great city and the
shipping in the bay (to be witnessed from the ob-
servatory; the magnificent trees, lovely walks; the
brilliant flowers and rare grasses, etc.,—and then
we said: *It pays to visit Woodward's Gardens.*

RETROSPECTION.

Thoughts of other days surround me,
   Wafted up by memory's flow;
Within my heart, they are sadly pointing,
   Back to Forty years ago.
Through the haze, and misty shadows,
   Wove by Time's unceasing tide,
I see the old familiar homestead,
   Where a loving Brother died.

And looking back a little farther,
   Voices sad, fall on my ear—
A group of little children gather—
   Bitterly weeping—'round a bier.
Faint and fainter, grow the voices,
   'Round that pallid form of clay;
And even now, I hear the whisper:—
   "Our Mother—she has passed away."

Years since then have come and vanished,
   Leaving in their rapid flight,
Hopes for future, by the way-side,
   That bloomed in Morn to fade at Night;
And now I find me looking backward,
   Through the dreary space, so wide—
Through the thickening, hazy curtains—
   To the day when Mother died.

O! how fond is memory's pleading,
   With our hearts, grown rude and cold;
Causing us to retrace our foot-steps,
   To the scenes in days of old.
Bringing up fond recollections,
   Of cherished ones, "gone on before—
Reminding us that we are nearer—
   Closer to the "other Shore."

FROM CALIFORNIA TO OLD MISSOURI!

A CHANGE OF CLIMATE APPEARS TO BE NECESSARY.

FOR SUCH IS LIFE.

This chapter, or sketch, I copy mainly from printed extracts taken from my old j o u r n a l, written at the time the events connected therewith were transpiring; and I publish it, as an illustration, to show that "man born of woman, is of few days, and full of"—changes.

Soon after reaching California, the second time, I went to Sebastopol, at which place I found my old companion, Reed, who had left Iowa several years before, and had, as he expressed it, "Come back to California to *stay*." I located in Santa Rosa, purchased a half interest in t h e Santa Rosa *Press* (it has since been changed to the *Republican*), but my health did not improve —in fact, within six weeks after my arrival in the Golden State, I became so reduced that I was ashamed to be weighed, and had to put *shot* in my pockets to induce the scales to gauge my weight at 112 pounds. I grew alarmed. An eminent physician advised me to change climate *at once*, and recommended *South-west Missouri!*

When I get scared, I act *promptly*—always did. I sold out my interest in the newspaper business, and six o'clock on Friday evening, October 16th, 1874, found the Author and his family o n t h e Oakland ferry-boat—crossing the Bay, to t a k e the cars at Oakland—enroute for the c o u n t r y East of the Rockies.

Out upon the waters of the grand old Bay, we take a long, lingering look at San Francisco. The night was beautiful—bright moonlight, calm and pleasant. A thousand brilliant lights were dancing and shimmering in the city; and thickly studding the harbor, rose the tall masts of s t a t e l y ships, and floating from their mast-heads the colors of almost every nation on the civilized globe—and the grim war sentinels, peering over the frowning battlements of Fort Alcatraz, all served to form a picture of more than ordinary magnificence and grandeur, and one that I shall look back to with pleasure, long after the incidents of the way shall have faded into forgetfulness. But this will never do. Sentiment must give way to solid facts and square built figures. We reached the train—everybody admits that— and soon had the satisfaction of finding ourselves snugly ensconced in good, comfortable s e a t s, which, by-the-way, is a most notable event in the journey overland, and in this case we were indeed fortunate in finding a large train, plenty of passenger cars and a small crowd.

We occupied the hind-most passenger car, and while we are munching crackers and passing peanuts around to our children, let us take a brief look at the occupants of our traveling coach, and find out if we can who they are and their reasons for going East. In the first place, close beside us is Mr. Peter Sweet and his wife. They had been to Oregon in search of health and a little more money, but, finding neither at an alarming rate, they were bound for their old home near Kalamazoo, Michigan, expressing a disgust for everything pertaining to gloomy, rainy, dismal, misrepresented Oregon.

There is Mr. Scott and family, going to their old home in Iowa. They had been living in San Jose, Cal., for some time; and were favorably impressed with California climate, with the exception of the *rainy season* and the *dry season;* and California having nothing else to offer in the shape of *seasons*, the Scott family had concluded to "rise and explain" to their friends in Iowa.

Scott was one of the most persistent ham eaters, I think I ever saw; he, aided by his amiable wife and a small corps of infantry, managed to "get away" with a whole ham about every second day—he was decidedly a "ham-fed man," and was going where pork could be successfully grown.

Then, there was a young, jovial Canadian, who had been in Oregon, Washington Territory, and

around Puget Sound considerably; he had grown
weary of a hard life and threadbare society, and
was going to where he would have a chance to
hear from the Lord at least once a week—he was

"marching down to old Quebec."

There was an Englishman from Nevada; and
he had his pockets filled with, what he termed:
moss "*hagets*" (no doubt meaning moss agates;)
and he had a great deal to say about *hog-den*. I
presume our English friend had reference to Ogden. This man had lost all faith in Nevada, and
was heading for Paterson, New Jersey. His first
name was John Mills.

In an adjoining seat, perched in an artistic attitude, was a quiet looking German, w h o h a d
spent six years in San Diego; and now he w a s
leaving glorious, s u n n y California, enroute for
New York, all on account of an enfeebled pocket
book and failing health.

A little farther on, we find Mr. Laufman and
his two sons.   They were from Plumas county,
Cal., and were going on a visit to their old home
in Illinois; and they were the only persons on our
car, who expressed their intention to return t o
California.

Then, we had a "wild Irishman" on board; he
had been digging and delving around San Francisco for a long time, when finally, no doubt, be-

coming too familiarly known at the *free s o u p houses*, he wrote to his "darlin' Biddy" to s e n d him the requisite number of "Spinner's auto-graphs," and now, he was heading for the East river; and lastly (ourselves excepted), there was a smart looking, old man, who had been throw-ing away his muscular development at San Le-andro, (or, as he termed it "Sallyander"), for seven years—doing his level best to earn enough to carry him to

"a low green valley on the old Kentucky shore."

But the adverse winds and fickle tides of for-tune had kept him on the threshold of the poor-house, until recently he had struck pay-dirt in a *one-horse Livery Stable*, at the rate of seventy-five cents a day; and now, he was going home to "play on a harp of a thousand strings." This man had lived eighteen years in Mobile—and he wanted everybody to know it.

He told every man, woman and child on the train, that he had "lived Eighteen years in Mo-bile;" and the funniest part of it was, he was con-tinually engaged in argument, upon a l m o s t all subjects, with which he was just as familiar as a *red rooster* is with a set of buggy harness— he wound up all arguments with the clinching as-sertion: "Gentlemen and Ladies, I know what I am talking about, for I have lived Eighteen years in Mobile."

This old San Leandro-ite told everybody—all along the route—from Sacramento clear to Omaha that he had "lived" 18 years in the city of Mobile; and by the time we reached Omaha, Nebraska, there were at least eighteen hundred and seventy-five individuals, who were familiar with the fact that we had on our train a m a n who had "lived in Mobile for Eighteen years."— This fact should be generally known.

On Sunday morning we crossed the line between California and Nevada, and soon a f t e r, reached Reno—292 miles from San Francisco, and, like a majority of home-sick emigrants, I soliloquized about as follows, as I stood on the platform of the car, watching the Sierras fading in the distance: We have left California behind us; California—the hardest country to get into, and the hardest country to get out of after you do get there. California—the fairest spot on earth when viewed through retrospective glasses, two thousand miles away! Thousands of people have expressed themselves in this manner—and afterwards changed their minds, just as I did, for in less than one year after my return to the 'States,' I found myself closing my eyes to the toil, trials and disappointments experienced on the Pacific coast, and in my mind's eye, beheld only those grand old mountain ranges, the green valleys— the crystal lakes and rippling streams of *beautiful California!*.

Reno is a beautiful town, situated at the Eastern base of the Sierra Nevada mountains. The Truckee river flows almost directly through the place. It is only 24 miles from Virginia City, and occupies quite an important railroad position.

In the valley near Reno, I saw several fields of Alfalfa, which is said to do well in that locality. A heavy-bearded, revolver-jeweled Reno-ite told me that the alfalfa in that region had but o n e root; and, said he, "that root will go down in the earth until it reaches water, if it has to bore its way clear through the Great American Desert— set up edge-ways." Rather than contradict him, I merely added—jes-so.

About twenty-five miles East of Reno, we enter the Great Desert—sixty miles of white sand, with only a stunted sage-bush now and then to relieve the monotony. Some people living in the *waste places* so frequently found along the Overland route, claim that all the country lacks, is— *plenty of water and good society.* As it has been intimated that those essentials are about all that *hell* lacks, we naturally conclude to locate *farther East.*

A considerable portion of this most desolate region was once inhabited, or rather *infested*, by the Shoshone Indians, whose chief occupation was murdering, and robbing; but after the Railroad—the world's great civilizer made its appear-

ance, the Indians were relieved of a great responsibility (so I have been told), and have been forced to take a back seat, in "beggars' row" and
"starvation corner." Once more—such is Life.

Leaving Nevada, we enter Utah, and after going about 125 miles, we reached Promontory, the
place that witnessed the completion of this great
Railroad; for it is at this point where the U. P.,
and the C. P. Railroads met—and the East and
West shook hands. We think it was the 10th of
May, 1869, when the last rail was laid, and the
last spike was driven—the event being witnessed
by nearly one thousand people, representing every State and Territory of this Republic. The last
spike (a gold one, presented by the State of California), was driven by ex-Governor Stanford.

Shortly after leaving Promontory, we come in
sight of Great Salt Lake. Away off to the right,
we see it, spread out like a vast inland Sea. The
landscape in this region, bordering the Lake, between Promontory and Ogden, is of rare beauty.
The land is very productive, and is mostly laid
out in small, well improved farms, and pure water is abundant.

As it will not do to tarry too long in Utah, we
will hurry on to Cheyenne—nearly 1400 miles
East of San Francisco. Here we laid in a supply
of venison and antelope; and then, after passing
over about fifty miles of the gradual descending

plain, dotted with an occasional farm house, vast
herds of cattle, and innumerable prairie dog vil-
lages, we enter the State of Nebraska. The general aspect of this State, is broad, rolling prairies.
The Western portion has rather poor soil, adapted principally to grazing, but the soil greatly im-
proves as we travel East.

Fifty miles farther, brings us to Sidney, and
then about fifty miles more, and we reach the old
town of Julesburg: and then we bowl along, following the course of the South Platte for nearly
seventy miles, until we reach North Platte City.
The country from Julesburg to North Platte is
much of a "sameness"—a fine agricultural and
grazing region, and is already yielding golden re-
turns to the hardy settlers.   One mile East of
North Platte City, we cross the North Platte river; and a short distance South of this, the North
and South forks of the Platte unite and form one
broad, but shallow stream, whose course we follow for nearly 250 miles, when it receives t h e
waters of the Elk Horn river, then diverges to
the right and joins the Missouri at Plattsmouth,.
fifty miles South of Omaha.   We first made the
acquaintance of the North Platte river at Fort
Steele, in Wyoming—more than 400 miles West
of North Platte City. Its length is supposed to be
not less than eight hundred miles. The great valley of the Platte is a magnificent region, almost
as boundless as the ocean.

One hundred miles farther East, and we reach
Kearney, and now we begin to catch glimpses of
old-fashioned civilization—poultry, hogs, patches
of corn and pumpkins, and log huts. (This was in
1874, please remember).

Thirty-five miles farther East, and Grand Island heaves in view. Grand Island, from which
the town derives its name, is the largest island
in the Platte river. It is about 40 miles long and
in many places, 2 miles wide. A bridge, eighteen
hundred yards in length, spans the Platte at this
point. In '74, Grand Island contained about two
thousand inhabitants, and as late as the winter
of 1880–'81, I was offered eighty acres of excellent land, all cultivated, within less than 2 miles
of the town, for *two hundred and fifty dollars!* The
party who owned the land, wanted to come to
California, *to raise oranges;* and at that time, I
was endeavoring to sell a printing office in Lincoln (Neb.), *for the same purpose.* Two fools met,
and *we did not trade.* (Please don't noise this af-
fair over all creation, for I am *weary.* Grand Island now, (1885), contains nearly ten thousand
inhabitants, with fine public school buildings,
churches, a Government Land office, Railroad
machine shops, large flour mills, &c.

Fifty miles East of Grand Island, we r e a c h
Loup City, and from here to Omaha—a distance
of nearly one hundred miles, it is difficult to im-

agine a more beautiful country—matchless prairies, interspersed with clumps of timber, thrifty
farms and flourishing towns, greet the eye on
every hand—along the entire route.

From Omaha, West, one hundred miles, and
from the same point, East, for the same distanre,
through Iowa, we can safely say, without fear of
contradiction, that Nature has been most lavish
in dispensing her rarest gifts, for, scarcely anything is lacking that is calculated to invite people to settle, and make their homes in that truly
magnificent, beautiful and fertile region. But we
must resume our journey.

It was Sunday evening—our second S u n d a y
since leaving San Francisco. The moon shown
with unclouded splendor; and t h e glimmering
lights of a City in the distance, plainly indicated
that we were nearing Omaha—the Eastern t e r -
minus of the "Wild West."

The entire length of the U n i o n and Central
Pacific Railroad—stretching from Omaha to San
Francisco, is 1925 miles. The first rail was laid
in July, 1865, and on the tenth of May, 1869, the
last spike was driven, and the road pronounced
in running order. The road is protected by over
70 miles of snow-fences and more than 40 miles
of snow-sheds. This road has been critically examined by the ablest engineers in t h e country,
and they have given it the highest praise. Hav-

ing several times, traveled from Ocean to Ocean, we unhesitatingly pronounce the Union & Central Pacific Railroad, one of the best constructed, and one of the safest roads in America. Its bed is smooth and solid, and a lasting credit to the skillful engineers under whose supervision it was constructed.

We arrived at Omaha in a thankful frame of mind; and it may be in order to state that the occupants of "our car" all stopped at the *Railroad House.* This house was fitted up by the Railroad Company, especially for *emigrants,* and it is so arranged that it can certainly a c c o m m o d a t e more people of the same size than can possibly be accommodated in any other hotel in America, *of similar dimensions!* For accommodating a *large* number with a *small space*—first, last and all the time—I say: *Give me a Railroad hotel to stop in—* (for about a minute).

During our night's "stop-over" in Omaha, at the Railroad Company's Hotel, the chief damage that I sustained, was in climbing the stairway to our "bed-room." Nearly all of my coat buttons were *scraped off,* while *squeezing between the walls of the stairway;* but I do not blame the Railroad Company for this trivial occurrence—I lay the blame entirely on the *stairway.*

About three o'clock in the morning we w e r e awakened from our flea-bitten slumbers, in order to get ready to take the train for Kansas City— and I think we all answered to the first call.

Of course, we had our "camp equipage" to get into shape for the journey, and in the hurry and confusion, the Author of this Book, packed his bundle rather "loose and careless," and after getting partly under it, I made several ineffectual attempts to rise with the enormous bundle, but was compelled to call the family to my assistance, and with a heroic and prolonged *"All together,"* I was enabled to assume an upright position, and then I staggered blindly in the direction of our train. It was very dark, and I had proceeded but a few steps, when my foot struck against the railroad track—and I *commenced falling*—and never let up until I fell over nearly one-third of the depot grounds, and finally came down, *all in a heap*, with less than half a ton of miscellaneous "trumpery" piled all around and on top of me. My first inclination was, to implore the first passer-by to bury me where I fell, but the puffing of an engine in close proximity to my head, caused me to abandon my first intention, with an agility that was really surprising. I threw blankets, tin pans, buckets, pillows, bread, fruit jars, and canned goods, right and left, and—arose. By rallying a few of our former fellow-travelers, a portion of my scattered luggage was recovered, and we finally managed to get on the train; and arrived at Kansas City without further mishap, and purchased tickets from there to Sedalia.

Our journey from Kansas City to Sedalia was made in the night, and of the appearance of the country, I am unable to give a lucid description, but in regard to the Missouri Pacific Railroad—between the two above-mentioned points—I will just say, that I never rode so fast, nor over such a rough road, or in such a crowded car, with less accommodations and courteous treatment, than on the night of October 26th, 1874, on the Missouri Pacific Railroad, between Kansas City and Sedalia. There were at least 150 persons crowded into the car we occupied. Every seat was jammed *more than full*; and the aisle was a surging, struggling mass of individuals, trying—o f t e n vainly, to keep on their feet. At least 25 passengers (many of them ladies), were compelled to crouch on the floor, huddle in the corners—or stand as best they could, in the passage-way, during the entire distance; and to add to the general discomfort—the night was warm—and the water-tank was *empty*.

Whether it was the badly proportioned coach, the rough road, or the rate of speed, I cannot say, but I never received such an unmerciful jolting, but once before—and that was over the rickety old rails that stretched from Nashville (Tenn.), to Chatanooga—in the stormy days of '63. But we reached Sedalia, without any serious ills, except skinned shins, lacerated pantaloons and "run-down" boots—all caused by desperate efforts to retain our footing on the car floor.

From Sedalia we went to Clinton, Henry county, where we located, and remained for one year, and would doubtless have made that our permanent home, but t h a t year—unfortunately, the grass-hoppers and chinch bugs took the contract for doing all the farming in that section of country—and we left the business in their hands, and moved to Crete, Nebraska.

In summing up my experience so far, in t h e Far West, I will just say: When I left California, I put it down as the most widely mis-represented country on the face of the Globe—*and perhaps it is.* I went there, *determined to like it;* but, for some cause or other, I soon found myself looking Eastward with a longing as fervent, as in former days I had looked upon the beautiful features of the Pacific slope. I am sometimes led to believe that this queer revulsion of feeling, after one *gets there,* is the result of a struggle (which nearly all experience), between the desire to remain; and the feeling of loneliness, and the kindred associations that are constantly urging us to return to our native haunts—and in about five cases out of seven, the latter wins!   .

When I had passed the Sierra Nevadas', on my return—as I beheld that quintessence of picturesque grandeur fading in the distance—I began to think California wasn't such a *hard country,* after all; and when in the great Nevada desert—

surrounded on every side with barrenness and desolation, the inward monitor of *discontent*, whispered in flattering tones, and pointed back to the
green valleys and shady nooks of California; and
while passing through Utah, I frequently found
myself telling loafers around the Railroad depots,
that, "California is no slouch of a place"—and
when I had passed Wyoming, all the disagreea-
ble features of the Pacific slope had, apparently,
simmered into fertility—the dust did not seem
half so deep—and the rainy season—it *wasn't so
very bad, after all!* And when I got down among
the papaw and persimmon patches, and "mud-
daubed" cabins of the Missouri River bottom, I
said to the natives: "Why don't you get out of
here, and go to California—and live like w h i t e
people?" During my year's sojourn in Missouri,
I really liked the appearance of the country, and
I am yet willing to admit, what I believe to be a
fact: that, considering her natural resources, Missouri is not much behind the first States of the
Union. With plenty of fertile land, an abundance
of timber, and inexhaustible mines of iron, lead
and coal, and a great river and its tributaries to
aid her commerce, it is yet a mystery to me why
land is held so cheap in many portions of t h e
State. In Missouri I found plenty of people who
were comfortably situated, trying to sell out, for
the purpose of removing to California! I had be-

gun to learn that *too much moving* was poor business, and resolved to do my level best to be contented and remain in Missouri; but after being
shook up with the ague a few times, singed with
lightning, pelted with hail-stones and half scared to death by deafening peals of thunder, I began to reflect. When the chinch bugs destroyed
the corn crop, I grew sad and somewhat dejected;
but when the grasshoppers came and commenced
to peel the apple trees and carry off the fence rails;
then I thought it was about time to draw a line,
and in drawing it, I drew myself and family out
of Missouri, and once more bent my steps Westward. (Shortly after I left Missouri, I understand
that the chinch bugs and grasshoppers also left,
and have not been there since! Reader, between you
and I, it is my candid opinion that I could make
a decent living if I was in old Missouri *now.*

HUNTING TURKEY ALONG THE OSAGE RIVER.

Verily, "Distance lends enchantment to t h e view," and I find myself drifting into my favorite theory, and that is: few of us know what we really want—and are seldom content when we have it.

A contented mind is the safest oar that ever paddled a life canoe adown the stream of man's earthly pilgrimage. If you are blessed with good health, and can make a good, honest living—stay where you are.

THE MARCH OF TIME.

Upon the golden span of To-Days's bright shore, we stand;
And, looking back, through Retrospection's vale,
Visions—sad, and beautiful—woven in Life's fitful dream, before us
    rise.
'Tis Spring, and over Earth, the queen of beauty walks.

Boyish foot-prints on hill-side, and in the vale, we see,
As though but yesterday they had been made;
And fancies of youthful days flit before us, with the same freshness
    —once so real,
Ere from our sight, they, by the remorseless flight of Time, were
    hurried.
A low-roofed cottage, with creeping vines, we see,
And down the beaten path, in front, a mother leads her boy.

                         Time rolls on.—
The Summer's heat and noon-day's sun have come and gone;
Autumn, with its "sere and yellow leaf" has tinged the forest trees,
Add given place to stern Winter, who holds the earth in fetters—
    cold and grim.

                          Years glide by.
Gone are the bright visions, and in their stead, we see a lonely grave,
And o'er it kneels a bent and aged form,
In whose shrunken eyes, we recognize the boy of long years ago—
And as the moaning wind goes by, we catch the meaning of his
    trembling voice,
As he sobs out the sacred words—"My Mother."

In one swift glance, we see how Life begins—and where the weary
  march will end.
A myth—a dream or vision, that one rude blast will e'en dissolve.
Nations by that invisible power, spring up and people the broad
  universe :—
Are born, and live—to droop and die !
And generations yet unborn, perchance, in future ages upon their
  graves will look, and wonder who within them lie.

The mighty warriors who guarded once the gates of Thebes,
Or lined the banks of the Euphrates—
Whose prowess for centuries kept the Eastern world at bay,
Had for their light, the same Sun, and Moon, and Stars, that we
  do now behold ;
And they, perchance, oft-times looked back to the foot-prints, and
Upon the resting place of their ancestors' dust.

Still onward sweeps the tide of years :—
Scepters, before whose imperial sway, nations paled—lie broken.
Empires, proud cities, massive gates and mighty walls, into decay—
Before the resistless march of Time, have crumbled.

To-day, a thousand fleets ride high o'er oceans' waves—
To-morrow, a thousand ghastly wrecks bestrew the shore ;
But Time, the great Tomb Builder, strides on ;
                                        His foot-steps never lag.
Suns rise and set ; and through the realms of space, glides the pale
  Moon—
Bathing in her silvery light, Mountains, Rivers and Plains that re-
flected her glances when first the world began.

                                        Seasons come and go,
Nor heed the fate of man, who with feverish brow and anxious tread.
Plods wearily through his allotted space, seeking, as it were, a place
  —to die.
But, thank God, a Hope—gathering strength from that golden
  promise—within our hearts shines forth :
Whispering of a fairer land than this, for those who love the Lord—
And from whence there'll be No Looking Back.

THE AUTHOR'S OPINION OF CALIFORNIA
AND OTHER STATES.

EVERY CLOUD is supposed to have a silver lining, and every picture, its bright side—and there
are, generally, two sides to every question.

Reader, we believe there is a sunny spot in every human heart, and we believe there is something good and noble in the nature of every man
"born of woman;" and we also believe there is
something good and and honest in every c i v i l,
political, and religious organization.   This rule,
we think, also applies to communities, States and
Nations.

Every Country, every State, and every district
has its advantages, as also its disadvantages; and
from my personal observations, during several
years residence on the Pacific coast, I feel justified in saying that California forms no exception
to the general rule.   And what I say, concerning
California, or any other State or country, I shall
endeavor to say—not from a desire to please any
particular class or community—but from an honest desire to deal fairly and squarely with my
fellow-men—and to tell the TRUTH, though the
Heavens fall!

When I first came to California, I had three objects in view: Health, Adventure, and a *Soft* quartz ledge: but finding neither to any great extent, after two years, I returned to the "States," thoroughly disgusted with everything pertaining to the far Western country—and strange as it may appear, since that time, I have repeated the journey from the East to California, FOUR times, each time bringing my family along and taking them back with me—and I am in California TO-DAY; and much of the time during my sojourn on this coast, I have been financially "busted," and often "out of flour!"

While in Nebraska, with the fierce storms of winter howling around me, I have often said: "Only give me standing room in California, and you can have my entire interest in all the country East of the Rocky Mountains—it's climate that *I* want." And often while in California, I might have been heard to exclaim: "Talk all you please about the sweeping winds and twisting "b l i z-z a r d s" of Nebraska, but the withering cyclone of poverty, so often felt in California, is the hardest wind I ever faced."

I have been repeatedly asked for an honest and impartial opinion in regard to California, and the prospects for a man bettering his condition by changing his location from the far East to the far West, but, owing to my being engaged in the

newspaper business during the greater portion of
my time while on the Western Coast, it has been
a very difficult matter for me to answer these im-
portunities—but I generally told my correspond-
ents to come and see for themselves; and I cannot now think of any better advice to give them.
I yet think and believe that it is best to deal honestly with our fellow-men, even if they do come as
strangers, with plenty of money, seeking homes
in a new location.

Now, we all know that just so long as T i m e
lasts, people will come to California—and go back
to where they came from; and many of those persons will repeat the operation (just as I h a v e
done), until they become financially demoralized,
and all that I write, *pro* or *con* upon the subject,
may have little or no effect upon the "moving"
class, for in nine cases out of ten, they will take
their own heads for it any way.

But notwithstanding all this, I propose to say
something for the benefit of those individuals
who have never been on the Pacific coast, a n d
who have their minds bent upon coming—no
matter what the sacrifice may involve;and my advice, honestly and sincerely given, is this: If you
and your family (if you have a family), are enjoying good health, and making a decent living,
do not sell out your old homes, and rush to California, with the expectation of bettering y o u r

condition, merely upon the strength of what you have heard. It is often easier to make a mistake than to correct one.

If, however, you are *determined to come*—then by all means, come before you sell out, and after you get here, do not be in too big a hurry, but take a good, careful look, and "see how it is your-self." If, after coming, you should conclude to remain, you will lose nothing by adopting this course; and upon the other hand, if you find the Pacific coast country does not meet your expectations, and find yourself disappointed, and consequently dissatisfied—then you will be doubly repaid in having pursued this common-sense policy of first taking a "look before you leap." And this rule applies, not only to the emigrant who seeks a home on the shores of the Pacific, but also to him who seeketh a new location in any portion of God's green earth!

I write this article for the benefit of the People who have their homes all over the broad land —and especially people in moderate circumstances—for the "common people" are the class who suffer most when disappointed by a change in location, and my sympathy naturally goes out to them in preference to the wealthy class, who are more able, and can better afford to endure reverses and disappointments.

Let me illustrate:

"A man from *our* neighborhood went to California several years ago, and in a short time, he struck "pay dirt"—came home rich, and bought the best farm in the county!"

Reader, you have no doubt heard about t h a t man—of course you have. He lived, not only in *our* neighborhood, but also in *your* neighborhood.

In fact, that same man, or another man just like him, lives, or has lived in almost every neighborhood East of the Missouri river—and I take it for granted that you have heard all about him. But did you ever hear anything about those *fifty* men who went from "our respective neighborhoods" to California, and struck *a different kind of dirt*—and did not make a fortune worth a cent, but who, on the contrary, got poorer day by day, and would have starved to death, had not the charitable institutions of San Francisco kept them alive until their friends in the East sent t h e m money to enable them to get back home?

Those fifty men lived in *my* neighborhood and also in *yours*! But history and real estate agents, and even the festive newspaper—aye, and society too, have been peculiarly silent in regard to the sad fate of those poor, unfortunate—misguided YOUTHS.

In many portions of the country over which I have traveled (in the East and West), I have observed one thing *i. e.*, all the good things of this world are seldom found together. On the contrary, I have frequently found good water, plenty of of fire-wood and poor soil, in *close communion*; and where there is *no sickness whatever*, you may just set it down that *nobody lives in that neighborhood!*. It is my candid opinion that this is an unhealthy world—and very few people ever get out of it *alive!*

The *best climate* in this or any other civilized country can generally be found in a newspaper or real estate office. (This is a fact that should be generally known).

California, in some respects, is a queer country. Some people, after coming here, like it very much, while others seem greatly disappointed— and consequently dissatisfied. I presume the way they succeed in "getting along" has much to do in shaping the minds of a great many individuals the world over.

Fruit of nearly every description, such as apples, peaches, pears, plums, prunes, apricots, nectarines, grapes, oranges, lemons, figs, &c., are all successfully grown; English walnuts and almonds also do well. Vegetables of all kinds are also grown to perfection, and attain an enormous size in favored localities.

Land in favored localities is held at very high figures—ranging all the way from fifty to three, four and five hundred dollars per acre, according to location, quality and improvements. I have known small fruit ranches of five and ten acres each, to sell for eight hundred and even a thousdollars per acre. It must, however, be remembered that such places are supposed to yield fruit to the amount of from one to three hundred dollars per acre each year.

The cheaper grades of land in the best portion of the State—that is, within reach of market, is, generally speaking, on the steep order—(set up edgeways), and requires considerable labor to clear it and bring it into proper shape for cultivation. Such land can yet be had at prices ranging from ten to thirty dollars per acre. When a new comer—or any other man, buys cheap land in California, he should endeavor to keep his upper lip stiffened with the encouraging reflection that, while he may have paid really more than the land is worth, he got "piles" of *climate*—all thrown in for nothing!

I do not wish to be understood as even attempting to write a history of any portion of California and its resources; and while having been over a considerable portion of the State from its Northern part to as far South as San Buenaventura— forty miles North of Los Angeles, I only claim to be familiar with the general features of Nevada, Yuba, Sacramento, Sonoma, Marin, Santa Clara and Santa Cruz counties; and will endeavor to confine myself to such facts as have come under my personal observation—such as I trust may be of interest, and possible benefit, to the general reader—and more especially the reader who has never seen California.

Wood, for fuel, especially in the northern and central part of the State, is plentiful—the prices in the principal towns ranging from four to nine dollars per cord; transporting the wood from the hills and mountains is where much of the cost is attached. In the Southern part of the State, timber is much scarcer and consequently fuel is considerably higher-priced, but the temperature is warmer, and less is required.

The kind of wood chiefly used for fuel in California, is redwood, madrone, white oak, chaparral roots, fir and live oak. Redwood is the cheapest, chaparral roots, white oak, madrone and fir come next in order, live oak being considered the best.

The counties bordering the Sea, as far South as Monterey, contain immense bodies of redwood timber, which produces the finest quality of lumber for building purposes, also, shingles, pickets, shakes, rails and posts. Having been through the most extensive forests of Sonoma and Santa Cruz counties, I am fully impressed with the idea that some day, not far distant, redwood timber will be as valuable property as the State contains—although some individuals seem to think the supply is inexhaustible. But when the fact is taken into consideration that an army of sturdy woodmen are constantly engaged in chopping in this timber, and hundreds of big saw-mills are cutting into it night and day—keeping ships, railroad trains, and countless teams constantly employed in transporting it North, South, East and West, it is not difficult to realize the fact, that redwood timber will yet be an object sought after in California. In fact, it is already steadily increasing in value. The soil in which the redwood trees flourish, is generally, if not always, of a superior quality; and the water in their vicinity, is always pure, cool and delicious.

Timber and building material of all kinds—also beef, pork and mutton, command about the same prices as in the more Eastern or Middle States, while butter, eggs, milk and poultry, as a general rule, command a higher price. Fruit and vegetables, as a rule, are sold by the pound; apples, peaches, pears and grapes, ranging from one to three cents per pound.

Mechanics wages range from two to four dollars per day; experienced miners receive from three to four dollars per day. Common laborers receive from one to two dollars per day. House rent is much the same as farther East.

The above, I consider a pretty correct statement; and I think it costs the common laboring classes a trifle more to live in California than it does in Illinois, Iowa, Missouri or Nebraska—at least, such has been my experience.

Some of my California readers may take exceptions to the above summing up, but I think the facts in the case will justify the statement—and as I am a resident of California (and hope to be for some time to come), and my interests all being here, should be sufficient evidence that I have no "axe to grind."

In speaking of the "common classes," I refer to those who, as a general rule, are unable to own land, and are compelled to labor for others—by the day, week or month, to procure the necessaries of life—and this class (God help them), are to be pitied in every land.

The common labor, for men, in California, is mining, farming, dairying, gardening, cultivating orchards and vineyards, driving teams, sawing logs, chopping wood, picking fruit, &c., with an occasional opportunity of packing your blankets and tramping in search of "something better."

I have received a great many letters from parties living East of the "Rockies," containing the inquiry: "What can a poor man do in California?" In answer to this inquiry, I can only say: that at this writing, the impression seems to be prevalent on this coast, that, owing to the presence of so many Chinese, with their cheap labor and economical mode of living—all the poor laboring classes of white people in this sunny land are doomed, sooner or later, to suffer the pangs of starvation. If this is the case, actuated by the spirit of charity, I would respectfully advise our "poor man" in the East to remain where he is— at any rate, until the Chinese have abandoned the Pacific coast.

My solution of the Chinese question is just the same as that of any other evil: Stop patronizing and supporting an evil, and that evil will soon cease to exist in your midst.

The climate of California is *Immense*—at any rate, I have been so informed by a particular and highly esteemed friend of my wife's uncle. Well, it's a fact, all the same. Tornadoes, wind-storms, snow and thunder and lightning are of very rare occurrence. In many portions of the State, there is scarcely wind enough during the entire year to blow a straw hat off a man's head—that is, of course, if he is the right kind of a man.

During the year there are perhaps, as many as three hundred bright clear days; during the remainder, it is either raining or liable to rain.

There are but two seasons in California:—the Dry season and the Rainy season.

The rainy season usually commences in November, and continues at intervals until March or April. Grain is sowed any time from October to April, according to the season. Plenty of rain in November, December, January and February, insures good crops.

The average rain-fall in San Francisco for the past thirty-five years has been about thirteen and one-half inches, varying from five inches (in '51 and '52), to twenty-eight inches (in '61 and '62).

Flowers bloom and plants of nearly every variety grow and flourish in the open air the year 'round; and vegetables of all kinds can always be had—fresh from the gardens.

In many portions of California, the scenery is grandly magnificent, and beautiful beyond description; and this, with the genial climate, has done much to cause the tourist and home-seeker to set their faces in the direction of these storied shores of the Western Sea. But the contemplating emigrant—especially with limited means at his disposal, must bear in mind the fact, t h a t SCENERY and CLIMATE alone, are "mighty" poor food for a hungry family. Of course, it may do for awhile, but for a *steady diet*, baked beans will *beat scenery two to one!* This is partly the Author's opinion.

For me to attempt to give the reader a full and complete description of California, in regard to her natural resources:—her wonderful productions—the mighty forests, the immense mining industries, the enchanting scenery and bewildering climate—would be somewhat like an elephant trying to climb to the Moon on a cobweb ladder, or like a poor man trying to make himself

popular in a wealthy and aristocratic neighborhood—or like the editor of a country newspaper
pleasing all his patrons. Those things are all to
be classed among the impossibilities.

It is well known that California is rich in min-
eral resources; but the "flush" days for the common miner have long since passed away.

The big claims that pay "thousands" are controlled by capitalists, who must necessarily be
wealthy in order to work the mines successfully;
and now it is the same in California as it is in
other countries:—the unfortunate *many*, work at
low wages for the fortunate *few*.

The counties bordering the coast, I consider as
the most suitable for homes. Wheat, oats and
barley are raised in immense quantities—and in
fact, almost everything that can be raised in any
country, can be successfully grown here.

The orange groves of Southern California are
yielding handsome revenues to their fortunate
owners; and the vineyards—scattered over the
State, will at no distant day, equal and perhaps
surpass the famous regions of the Rhine; while
orchards—on the mountain tops, on the hill-sides
and in the valleys, bend beneath their burdens
of delicious fruits, that find a hearty welcome in
every market of the civilized globe.

But of course, kind reader, this is the bright side of the picture. All these good things a r e here, but it takes money—*and lots of it,* to buy a good revenue-paying home in California! And while it is true that the soil in portions of California is capable of producing as much as eighty bushels of wheat to the acre, it must also be borne in mind that at least three-fifths of the e n t i r e State does not contain enough genuine soil to produce second-grade dog fennel or respectable cactus.

A great many old residents say: "The climate isn't like it used to be—the soil doesn't produce so well—the rainy season cannot be depended on, and disease, too, with its pale and shadowy forms is creeping in, gaining a foot-hold in the lovely valleys—along the hill-sides, and on the mountains of this classic land."

How all this is, I will not say, for I have often heard similar complaints in States East of California—for there are grumblers everywhere.

Some people seem to forget what *has been,* and are harder to please as they grow older. Few of us truly appreciate the blessings of TO-DAY, and seldom know when we are at *home.* HOME! How I have learned to love that word, as I look back over the homeless wastes through which my restive feet have wandered.

Although far advanced in the walks of civilization, yet, of the world's teeming millions, how few there are who know how to be happy—or if they do know, how few utilize their knowledge by striving to secure the priceless boon?

Reader in the far East, if you are a poor man, let me impress the fact upon your mind, that it is a very risky business to move with a family, two thousand miles in search of "something better," at least, without first taking a look over the field. I have tried it FOUR different times, and I ought to be tolerably well posted on the subject. But it does not cost much to travel. Paying for your tickets is what takes the money!

Of one fact I am perfectly assured, and that is: During the past twelve years, I have scattered a snug little fortune in cash, between Omaha, Nebraska and San Buenaventura, California, and have nothing to show for that cash except some old Railroad and Steamboat receipts, s h o w i n g when and where a certain individual (well known to the Writer), had paid so much, for freight on household goods, printing material, Etc., Etc.— Yes, I have something else left to remind me of my scattered fortune:—*experience!* I have "piles" of that, and by giving the public the benefit of it, if *one poor family* can be kept from squandering a *home*—which took years of toil to make—as I have done, I will look back with pleasure, upon at least that portion of my life's labors.

Rich or Poor, a contented mind is better than Gold. It is almost everything worth living for in this world. It is the gate-way to Health, Wealth and Happiness.

The journey to California has disappointed and financially ruined more people than it has ever *enriched, satisfied* or *bettered.* And I feel justified in saying, that he who leaves a good home East of the Rocky mountains, with a heavy heart—a discontented mind and a restless, roving disposition, basing his move upon the expectation of bettering his condition, will rarely, if ever, find on the Pacific coast, that which he seeketh—for "All that Glitters is not Gold."

SITTING BULL REVIEWS THE SITUATION
THE DAY BEFORE CHRISTMAS.

Children of the West: Listen to the voice of your Chief. It is Sitting Bull that speaks. The Thomashawk is buried—the healing aroma of the calumet floats over the camp. It has been many Moons since I have addressed you in festive words, but the Christmas time is upon us, and Sitting Bull don't care for incidental expenses.

To-day we stand mid the mouldering ruins of a dying year—and not one of us can help it!

The "sere and yellow leaf" is 'round about our camp. The nights of our discontent and scarcity of Government blankets hover near.

Many of us have passed over the "summit," and are gradually nearing the Western horizon of our earthly existence. Many Summers ago, we were children, and hailed the approach of the Holidays with delight. Since that time, many

Suns have risen and set; and we have wandered from the yellow waters of the Mississippi to the sands of the Pacific. *We* have grown old, but a host of children play around our wigwams to-day. Let us remember them when we go home to-night. Let us fill up every little stocking in the camp. It will make the papoose happy. It will make us better Indians. It will bring us closer to the Stars. It will make the Sun shine brighter. It will please your Chief, for he was once a child.

Children of the Occident:—my talk is nearly ended. The spirit of Santa Claus urges me to close, for—

> Soon it will be Christmas day,
> And my heart's so nearly full
> Of Good Will to my fellow-men,
> It "gets away" with Sitting Bull.

CALIFORNIA AND THE EAST.

To-night, as I sat thinking,
Of the difference in this clime,
And that of other countries,
My thoughts flowed into rhyme,
In the East, cold winds are blowing,
And snows are drifting high,
While poverty's child is shivering,
'Neath a cheerless winter sky.

From the "Rocky's" rugged ranges,
To Atlantic's flowing tides—
Through all that famous country,
Where the Mississippi glides—
In every City, town and hamlet,
With snow and ice on every hand,
There's a shivering and a shaking,
Over in that frozen land.

There sits the "old inhabitant,"
In the country village store,
Telling his forty-seventh lie:—
"It was never half so cold before!"
The Storm-King waves his sceptre,
Winds blow at his command;
And fires burn *down* while coal goes *up*,
Over in that frozen land.

But here in California,
    The grass is always green,
And flowers of brilliant colors,
    On every hand are seen;
Wild birds are singing sweetly,
    . As they flit from tree to tree,
And brooks go rippling merrily,
    On their journey to the Sea.

The air is soft and balmy—
    The skies are bright and clear,
And the "Winter of our discontent"
    Is "glorious Summer" here!
And, sitting here to-night, I wave
    My hat, with loving hand—
To all the shivering dwellers in
    The famous frozen land.

Los Gatos, California,
    February 5th, 1884.

RECOLLECTIONS OF SHILOH.

A SKETCH FROM MEMORY.

How TIME FLIES! It has been Twenty-three years ago, and yet it seems but a few days, since that wild hurricane of death swept over the great camp.

On the 6th and 7th of April, 1862, one of the most fierce and bloody battles of the Great Rebellion was fought. We refer to the battle of Shiloh—also familiarly known as the battle of Pittsburg Landing; and every year, when the 6th and 7th of April comes around, fancy leads me back to the historic spot; and the thrilling scenes connected with that eventful field, grow fresher in my memory as the years glide by.

I remember the great fleet of steam-boats that moved up the Tennessee river in the latter part of March, and tied up to the shore in the vicinity of Pittsburg Landing. This convoy of boats started from Savannah, (a small village about eight or nine miles below the Landing), where for several days they had been concentrating.

If I remember aright, there were nearly o n e hundred transports, each one carrying from five hundred to one thousand soldiers. These boats contained the flower of the Union Army of the West; and as they wended their way to their destination, no grander sight was ever witnessed on the waters of that beautiful river.

The grand array of steamers, the bright uniform, the glistening bayonets, gleaming sabres— the inspiring strains of martial music, and that mighty array—over whose veteran legions, the glorious ensign of our Country proudly floated— all served to form a panorama such as has s e l- dom been witnessed in a life-time.

I remember our "going into camp" away out in the fields and upon the hills and slopes above the river—the camp of the Grand Army extend- ing from right to left for the distance of nearly five miles, the flanks resting nearer to the river, while from the Landing to the front and centre of the army the distance was in the neighbor- hood of from four to six miles. (This interval be- tween the army and the river was greatly dimin- ished before the sun set on Sunday evening, Ap- ril 6th).

I remember the long trains of artillery (heavy siege guns and field batteries), and the clouds of cavalry, coming from Savannah, and taking their position in the camp.

At this camp the army was to remain for a few days in order to rest and make the necessary preparations for a grand advance against Corinth, Mississippi—distant a little over twenty miles.

This was only a short time after the fall of Fort Donalson; and never was an army more jubilant or confident in its strength and superiority than was the army of the Tennessee as it basked beneath the waving folds of the "old flag," in that grand encampment on the hills above the Tennessee river, opposite Pittsburg Landing, during those first few days of April, 1862—none dreaming that death was lurking so near. No one seemed to think, that before many hours m o r e went by, the Sun, the Moon and the Stars would be looking down upon that great camp—looking down upon the pallid faces and mangled forms of twenty thousand dead, dying and w o u n d e d soldiers!

I remember the grand review that took place (occupying the greater part of three days), April 3rd, 4th and 5th. Such a review has s e l d o m been witnessed on American soil. That army of the Tennessee represented a force of between sixty and seventy thousand men—including cavalry—with a full complement of Artillery, consisting of siege guns and field batteries.*

* Although I am not prepared to prove it, yet at the time, it was the general impression in camp, that the Union army had more than three hundred pieces of Artillery on the field of Shiloh.

The respective Brigades and Divisions w e r e commanded by men who were familiar with the art of war—for those gallant divisions were led, the first day on that fated field by Generals, Sherman, W. H. L. Wallace, Prentiss, Logan, Hurlburt, McClernand and Smith—all under the command of General U. S. GRANT; and on the s e c- o n d day of the fight they were aided by Generals, Lew Wallace, McCook, Crittenden and Nelson with their respective divisions—under the chief command of General Buell. What army, either before or since, can show a braver or more skillful leadership?

I remember the gala appearance of the camp—the Soldiers all busily employed in making preparations for the expected move against Corinth, at which place it was generally understood that the Confederate army was concentrated—l i t t l e thinking that the Southern host, even then, was massed in battle array, only a few miles distant —yet such was the case.

The morning of the 6th came around; and just about sunrise, a few random shots were heard a-way out on the "front." But the "boys" (many of whom were getting ready for breakfast) said: "It is the picket guard emptying their g u n s." But the firing continued—and increased as it continued—and a few minutes later, a cavalry-man,

mounted on a foaming steed, dashed through our
camp, startling us with the announcement that
the entire Rebel army was coming down upon us
in three heavy lines of battle—"and," he added,
"General Prentiss with nearly all of his command
has just been captured." And then, the hurried,
half whispered words: "*a surprise!*" * flew from
man to man; and soon the ominous sound of the
"*long roll*" could be heard away out on the front,
the drummers of one division after another taking up the battle call, until the dread notes rang
out from one end of the camp to the other, and
but a few moments had elapsed ere the suddenly
awakened soldiers were "falling in" and

"Swiftly forming in the ranks of war,"

and half an hour later, the Army of the Tennessee presented the front of

"Battle's magnificently stern array."

I remember hearing the orders that passed
from regiment to regiment—orders that w e r e
plain enough to be sufficiently understood by the
common soldiers to satisfy them that a terrible
battle was coming on; and but a short time suf-
ficed to reveal the fact that the combined army
of the South, under the command of Generals,
Beauregard and Albert Sydney Johnson, w a s

* I thought so at the time—have thought so ever since—and yet
believe—and all opinions to the contrary (no matter from w h a t
source they come), will never make me cease thinking and believ-
ing that the Union Army was completely SURPRISED by the Rebels,
at Shiloh on Sunday morning, April 6th, 1862.

sweeping down upon us like an avalanche, crushing everything before it.

I remember the hissing, screaming shells, the booming artillery, the incessant crash of musketry, and the horrible rumble and roar of the fierce conflict, as it deepened in the centre and thundered on the flanks.

I remember the thrilling events of that terrific day:—the furious storm of shot and shell—the crash of falling timber—the swift capture of entire batteries—the ghastly heaps of the dead and dying, and the sad moans, shrieks and supplications of the wounded—and all the time, the National army was being pushed slowly, but steadily, back towards the river.

I remember, about three o'clock in the afternoon of that terrible day, I beheld a vast portion of that mighty army of the Tennessee, shattered, broken a n d panic-stricken—rushing m a d l y, w i l d l y, in the direction of the river, with the storm of death closely following at their heels; and on the bank of the Tennessee river, I remember the heroic efforts, on the part of gallant officers, to rally this disorganized host, and the fierce and stubborn fighting that took place, when the panic-stricken soldiers found that the river cut off all retreat.

Those were the hours, during that first day's awful fight, when men from Illinois, Indiana, Iowa, Kentucky, Ohio, Wisconsin and Michigan, with bated breath, looked into each other's faces, and repeated the oft-asked question: "Where is Buell and his army?"

Two more dreadful hours went by—hours on which the fate of this Government seemed to hang trembling in the balance; the broken hosts of the Union had been forced back almost to the brink of the river—the hills and ravines were deluged with blood, and literally heaped with the dead and dying, and the Rebel host, flushed with apparent victory, were still advancing step by step.

At this critical moment, in fancy, I can yet see the two gun-boats—Tyler and Lexington, steaming swiftly to the rescue, anchoring at a favorable point, the smoke-blackened gunners stripped for action, and soon after, letting loose their "grim dogs of war," raining a perfect storm of shot and shell on the advancing Rebels. Yet, on they came, confident of securing a great victory, that seemed almost within their grasp!

But look! Just across the river, through the murky clouds of battle, the flags, glistening bayonets and the long, dark lines of Infantry, proclaim the joyful fact that Buell's long-looked-for army is near at hand—an army of thirty thousand fresh soldiers are hurrying to "Uncle Sam's" assistance! That was indeed, a supreme moment, and one never to be forgotten by the soldiers who stood on that bloody ground.

The glad news flew like the wind all over that vast field; thousands of soldiers in Grant's army who had lost hope, once more "rallied 'round the Flag," and a shout went up from the Army of the Tennessee that rose above the din of battle, and shook the eternal hills.

The remnants of Grant's army were rallied— the tide of battle was checked, and protected by a terrific rain of lead from the gun-boats, Buell's army crossed the river, and rushed into the fight.

Night closed over the scene, and the two hostile armies rested from their work of destruction, and laid down to sleep within talking distance of each other. But as soon as the first streaks of dawn heralded the approach of another day, a new line of battle was formed, Buell's forces taking the advance, and the bloody conflict was reopened by the Union army—the desperate fight continuing with unexampled fury until near one o'clock in the afternoon, when the Rebel army, after hours of the most desperate resistance, gave way, slowly and sullenly retreating to their former position at Corinth, leaving thousands of their dead and wounded on the field, and bearing with them the mangled corpse of their daring leader, Albert Sidney Johnson. Thus ended those two days of terrible fighting. The field of Shiloh was won, and Hope marched forward with quickened step to the music of the Union.

MY OLD CANOE.

'Twas Spring—the birds were warbling
    Their wild carols all around,
I left the home of boy-hood's years,
    For the Western country, bound.
The sun shone bright o'er fields of green,
    As I waved my last adieu—
And with swelling heart and dimming eyes
    I launched my Life canoe.

The deep Sea widened 'round my bark,
　Strange voices filled the air,
Even though, with strangers on the deep,
　I knew that God was there.
Time rolled on, and soon I stood
　On a distant Western shore—
California's soil beneath my feet,
　And her blue sky spreading o'er.

Two years sped by, and I awoke
　From that bright, golden dream;
And with my old Canoe, once more,
　I pushed out in the stream.
When angry waves and adverse winds
　All my efforts did deride,
I laid my wave-worn paddle down,
　And drifted with the tide.

My boat was shattered by the storms,
　And my hands were brown'd by toil,
I felt sure that welcome awaited me
　Upon my native soil—
And when I saw the dear old shore,
　Rise over the waters blue,
I knew that a landing place was near,
　For me and my old Canoe.

My boat now lies upon the shore
　Of Life's tempestuous stream,
While far above the stormy heights,
　I see the Light-House gleam.
My last great cruise I soon must take—
　To earth-land, bid adieu—
Then, into the mists of unknown seas,
　I will push my old Canoe.

CAPITAL VERSUS LABOR.

"THE time will come sooner or later when Capital and Labor will constitute the two great powers that will stand arrayed against each other in these United States; and instead of being Democrats and Republicans, it will be the Laboring classes and the Capitalists."

Sentences similar to the above, we hear almost every day, and while there may be some truth contained therein, so far as my experience goes, I am inclined to think, that to a greater or less extent, there has always been, and always will be a species of antagonism between capital and labor—not only in this, but in all countries—each party striving to gain positions and control circumstances which will enable it to place the other at a disadvantage, and compel an acceptance of the terms offered.

Capital to a very great extent, is the result of labor, and the more independent the producer becomes, the less the power of the capitalist over him. If labor is scarce in proportion to the demand, it becomes independent, and as a natural consequence it demands higher wages; when labor is in excess, it becomes dependent, and capital secures its advantage by reducing wages.

The voting power is really held by the laboring classes, but circumstances, too often control the majority and forces them to accept the terms and become the slaves of the money power.

The nearer these great powers are balanced, the better it is for the world at large, for either one is dependent upon the other; and let either representative get the "upper-hand," every advantage is speedily taken—for human nature is *human* nature, everywhere.

When the laboring classes begin to work, think and act for themselves—voting strictly on principle, keeping out of debt and living within their means, they will soon rear for themselves a platform, upon which they can proudly stand, and hold at arm's length, all the capitalists, corporations, monopolies and "scalpers" in creation.

OUT IN THE DARK,

—OR—

THE DRUNKARD'S SOLILOQUY.

OUT IN THE DARK, on the Drunkard's road,
   I am trudging along the way,
With scarcely a ray of hope beyond—
   And my hair fast turning gray.
For years, along Life's path-way,
   I have groped in fear and doubt,
While in the chambers of my heart,
   The Light seems going out.

I once was deemed the "foremost man"
   In all this country 'round—
And called "a public benefactor"
   By the people of the town:
Kind fortune smiled upon me,
   And left her golden mark;
But, too weak to stand temptation—
   I drifted in the Dark.

I've watched my fated star grow dim,
   Till it faded from my sight—
Amid the wreck of misspent years,
   While blacker grows the night.
Few, (save the wretched drunkard),
   Who on troubled seas embark,
Can ever realize what it is
   To be—out in the Dark.

The lines are deepening on my brow—
  I am "going fast" they say;
And the shadows thicken 'round me,
  As I stagger on my way.
My once loved childrens' prattle,
  Heard in the family arc,
Grows fainter in the distance—
  As I drift out in the Dark.

The grass will soon be growing
  Above us all, I know;
But my wife and children they will be,
  Where the father cannot go.
In a bright land "over yonder,"
  They will wear a shining mark;
While I, the wretched drunkard,
  Will be—out in the Dark.

I can feel my boat fast gliding
  In the shadows, cold and gray;
Comes again the fearful warning:—
  I am "passing fast away."
I can hear the billows dashing
  Against the Stygian shore;
But alas!—I see no beacon,
  To guide me safely o'er.

Memory's waves go surging past me—
  And hark! above the roar,
I can hear my children calling—
  From the fast receding shore;
The "Rum Fiend," that hideous monster,
  Sounds out the dismal knell,
That shuts me out from Heaven,
  And drags me down—to Hell.

What I Know About Raising Hogs.

I have frequently been asked the question:—
"Does it pay to raise hogs?" I unhesitatingly answer—Of course it does. I say this because I am
posted on the subject, at least, I have a v a g u e
idea that I know what I am talking about. If
the question was asked me: Does it pay to run a
newspaper in a small town? I might hesitate,
and perhaps request my interlocutor to give me
thirty days to consider the matter, and even at
the end of that time I might not be able to give
a decided answer; but when it comes to raising
hogs, I wish to impress the fact upon the mind
of the Reader that I know all about it, as the following illustration will show.

Once upon a time, not many years ago, while
engineering the running-gear of a small newspaper in a small village in the West, and realizing
the fact that the meat market was steadily ab-
sorbing the principal portion of my little business, I resolved to erect an independent platform.

In short, I resolved to "raise my own meat;" accordingly I purchased two pigs, which cost me four dollars. At the time I made this purchase I had in the neighborhood of half a ton of ground mill-feed on hand for my cow, and while t h a t mill-feed held out, the expense of keeping those two pigs did not amount to "a hill of beans," but after that was gone, I began to pay frequent visits to the mill, and also notified my subscribers that all who wished to, could pay their subscriptions in anything that a pig could "worry down," and in this manner I got even with a number of old delinquents.

Time drifted by, and at the end of two months I killed one of my small hogs, (done the job myself). I have never even *tried* to kill a pig since that time. Reader, between you and I, that pig was not merely *killed*, he was *murdered*! I am not a professional butcher. As near as I can recollect, with the aid of a shotgun, I inserted three charges of bird shot into that shoat's cranium, and wound up by sticking him at every available point, until finally he yielded up his young life, leaving me filled with regret in not having called in a marksman who could have brought him down at the second fire. The day after the massacre I walked by the butcher shop as independent as the man Vander built; and thinks I, Mr. Butcher, it will be "a cold day" when you sell the editor any more pork for the next long time or two to come. Vain thought! Reader, as sure as our National Holiday comes on the 4th of Juvember, we ate that entire shoat—head, feet, ears and all *in just five days!* Soon after this I sold the family cow, and made large investments in ground barley, ground corn, and almost every thing else that had any ground-work about it, for I was determined to make a hog out of the other pig. But why prolong this sad experience? Why linger over the fitful dream of misguided ambition? I will not linger. In the course of time, I sold the remaining shoat for eight dollars and seventy cents. Reader, let me whisper a word in your ear: *There is money in hogs!* I know this to be a fact, for I put about thirty dollars into one *pig!*

TAXATION AND CONVICT LABOR.

As this book is principally made up of separate sketches and miscellaneous articles, and as
this will probably be the last book the A u t h o r'
will be guilty of "kicking off" on a job press, I
wish to submit my humble opinion on the subject of Taxation and Convict labor.

The present system of taxation seems very un-
just in many cases. As it is, the principle favors
are given to the wealthy class, while the poor
class receive few favors and are taxed without
mercy. In my humble opinion no citizen whose
capital does not exceed one thousand dollars (be
it in land, stock or tools), should be taxed anything. One thousand dollars is a small capital
for any man to make a decent living for himself
and family.

There is sufficient property aside from the above mentioned class, if properly assessed and collected to accomplish the desired ends. There is no doubt in regard to this; but the trouble is, as a general rule, the wealthy class, the big corporations &c., are seldom assessed for half what they should be, and even then if the assessment does not suit them, they combat the enforcement of the laws, and often come out victorious. Thus the classes who are able to pay and who should be compelled to pay, get off with a light levy, while the poor man, who may be so fortunate as to be the possessor of two or three acres of land, is compelled to give in every item, even down to cow and chickens, and when tax paying day comes he gets no "three days of grace."

In this age, the problem of the poor man is: How shall I manage to pay my taxes this year? The problem of the rich man and the big corporation too often seems to be: What plan can I devise to deceive the assessor and shield my property from taxation? This may be plain talk. But where is the thinking man in this country who is not fully persuaded in his own mind that such is the case? The rich man is, and generally has been favored; and now why not give the poor man a chance, if it be no more than to lighten his taxation?

I also take the position that the manner of dealing with convicts is all wrong. My idea is, when a man is convicted of a crime and sent to prison for ten or twenty years, or for life, as the case may be, at least one-half of his earnings should be set aside and paid regularly to his family (if he has a family) or to those who may have been dependent upon him for support. Such a course as this, would be humane and Christian-like; and the knowledge of doing something—even though inside the walls of a penitentiary—to aid in the support of his family, would do more to soften that man's heart and make a better man of him, than all the coarse fare and rigid prison discipline that can be administered or enforced.

MY OLD E FLAT.

(I once had a great desire to become a member of a Brass Band; and that desire was gratified, but unfortunately, I selected an "E flat" horn, and thirteen days afterwards, I came out—at the "little end," tendered my resignation, and concluded to go West).

Show me the man in all this town,
Or even in the country around,
Where e'er he may be, or can be found,
   From a dandy flirt, that pride begat,
To a man or boy of any kind—
Who has an ample supply of wind,
   To blow my old *E flat*.   ·

Fetch 'round the lad, and I'll 'go for him,'
I will satisfy his every whim,
And through my paper I'll 'blow' for him,
   And on all occasions, pass 'round the hat,
To support his family in after years,
And keep the children from shedding tears,
   For father, who died (in *E* horn) so *flat*.

Oh! I would like to see with my own eyes,
The man who lives under Northern skies,
Who wishes upon the *"Air"* to rise—
Who is foolish enough, and all that,
To tarry long with this piece of brass,
Making a noise, resembling an ass—
Which is all I can do on my *E flat.*

There must be some reckless chap around,
In the country, or within this town,
In *wind* and *limb* "almighty" sound,
That would like to "smell a rat."
Show me the man—I'll give him a horn
That will make him sorry he was born,
In the days of my *E flat.*

They say this is a progressive age,
And every body has grown so sage—
To go ahead is all the rage;
They can all do "this and that."
But I want to see that man "for fun,"
Who by a horn can't be out-done;
He must be a perfect *"blow"* or none,
For it will take a regular "son of a gun"
To blow my old *E flat.*

DEATH OF MRS. JOHN BROWN.

(Copied from my Journal of March 7th, 1884).

THE WIDOW of John Brown, of Kansas fame and Harper's Ferry notoriety, died in San Francisco, California, on the 29th day of February, 1884. She was the second wife of "old John Brown," and the mother of thirteen children. Some years ago she purchased a mountain ranch near Saratoga, Santa Clara County, California, and here she lived in a quiet, unassuming way, with a daughter and son-in-law, until about one year ago, when she sold her ranch and purchased a small place near Saratoga, where she lived until her last visit to San Francisco (where she went for medical treatment—and where she died).

By her intimate neighbors, Mrs. Brown is spoken of as a quiet, hospitable and Christian woman, in whom religious duty of the Puritan character strongly predominated, and a woman with whom it was a real pleasure to converse.

Her remains were conveyed to Saratoga, and the funeral sermon preached by the Rev. W. H, Cross, from the text: "Well done, good and faithful servant."

About five hundred people attended the funeral (among whom were many members of the Grand Army of the Republic), and followed the remains to the grave.

Thus has passed away from earth, the widow of "old John Brown"—a name that is destined to live while the history of the Great Rebellion is read; for John Brown was certainly the first man to lay down his life on the altar of African liberty in the United States. His blood quickened the strife that soon after, deluged the land with human gore.

And, while we may not endorse the fanaticism that urged him on, we must admit that John Brown's action at Harper's Ferry, was the first blow that started the rivets from the chains that held four millions of human beings in bondage.

The great Civil War, doubtless would have come upon us sooner or later, but John Brown's raid, followed by his cruel execution, precipitated the struggle at least twenty years in advance of its natural solution.

As a scrap of interesting history we give the following extract from that wonderfully eloquent speech of John Brown to the Court that sentenced him to the gallows in December, 1859; and that is his authority for the capture of Harper's Ferry:

"This Court acknowledges, as I suppose, the validity of the Law of God. I see a book kissed here, which I suppose to be the Bible, or, at least, the New Testament. That teaches me "that all things whatsoever I would that men should do unto me, I should do even so to them." It teaches me further, to "remember them that are in bonds as bound with them." I endeavored to act up to that instruction. I say I am yet too young to understand that God is any respecter of persons. I believe that to have interfered as I have done—as I have always freely admitted I have done—in behalf of His despised poor, was not wrong but right."

The widow of "old John Brown" rests in peace, and in the beautiful Spring-time, when l o v i n g hands are weaving garlands to decorate the graves of the Nation's honored dead, let no one be ashamed to drop a tear of sympathy or to strew earth's fairest flowers on the grave where sleeps Mary A. Brown.

LINES TO "TOM BROWN."

(AN ARMY COMRADE).

Some twenty years ago, Tom Brown,
  I struck for the Western Sea;
And old-time memories prompt me now,
  To write these lines to thee;
For, no matter where I go, dear Tom,
  I am ready to proclaim :—
Our friendship nought on earth can break,
  And I know you'll say the same.

Tom Brown, the years go flitting by—
  Our work will soon be done;
Life's battle, fought by you and I,
  Will soon be Lost or Won!
And with old-time recollections,
  Swelling in my heart to-night,
I cannot refrain from asking :—
  Have we fought the Goodly fight?

Oft I think the World is changing,
  And the snares in this great land,
For weak and wayward mortals,
  Grow harder to withstand;
But oft our mode of living,
  Converts Morning into Noon :—
Makes Summer months to flee away,
  And Winter come too soon.

Tom Brown, while cherished memories,
　Flood my heart with golden light,
Days, months,—aye, years of that olden time,
　Spread out before my sight—
The tented field, the bivouac fires,—
　The tempest's angry frown—
And a cabin that sheltered two old friends :—
　Myself and Thomas Brown.

Though we may meet no more on earth,
　As in the days of yore,
They tell me there's a Better Land,
　Upon a Golden Shore !
And my heart grows strong within me,
　As adown Life's stream I row—
For in that bright land I hope to meet,
　Tom Brown—of the "Long ago."

CHRISTMAS CHIMES.

As the Christmas chimes peal out, we hear the merry shouts of the boys, the light ringing laughter of the girls, and the friendly, hearty greeting and cordial interchange of good feeling among the older folks. The Holidays seem to possess the rare charm of unlocking the icy channels and frozen natures of civilized nations, harmonizing the great human family, strengthening our good resolutions, making better men and better women all over the land.

Almost all of us have golden memories stamped upon the Christmas pages of long ago; and when our thoughts go back to our dear old fathers and mothers and our kind and loving brothers and sisters, as in fancy, we pass down the shadowy aisle of retrospection—above the ripples of busied memory, we catch the echoes of those old Christmas Chimes, and over the dim horizon of that golden age, the cheerful glow of the Christmas fires casts its hallowed light.

Reader, while summing up the many blessings which the Giver of all good has so bounti-
fully bestowed upon us, let us thank Him for
casting our lines in a land where the cheerful
chimes of Christmas ring out once a year; and
when the shadows of night have closed around
your Christmas pillow, may you feel deep down
in your heart that "Peace on Earth and Good
Will to all mankind"—even such as our Saviour
taught nearly two thousand years ago.

OUR FAVORITE SALUTATORY.

(As I have had the good fortune or misfortune to publish a newspaper in some half a dozen different places, I insert my old favorite and often used salutatory, having "fired" it off at the public —East and West—with good results. I give it a place in this book as I wish to preserve it for future reference, and possibly for future use.)

To the good people of this town and vicinity, and to all others into whose hands this paper may come, the editor lifts his battered tile from his *bald* forehead and makes his most respectful bow. In our salutatory we will endeavor to be brief and to the point.

We come comparatively a stranger in y o u r midst. We bring no reference to offer, nor do we wish any save what our efforts may justly entitle us to.

We bring a new and extensive printing outfit with us, and it belongs exclusively to us.

We come determined to solve what is considered by some individuals a debatable question as to whether or no this town is able and willing to support a weekly newspaper; and although we have been warned of the quicksands, up-grades and slippery places that so thickly be-strew the pathway of the man whose ambition p r o m p t s him to commence the publication of a newspaper in a small town, we launch our craft with the comforting assurance that "the battle is not always with the strong nor the race to the swift."

We have an abiding faith in the combination of industry, economy and perseverence; and our faith is strengthened by thoughts of the glorious future that surely await all legitimate branches of business in this classic region.

We propose to publish a newspaper devoted to home interests—to aid in building up this town and the region round about, to advance agricultural and manufacturing interests, and all other professions, institutions and branches of industry that will tend to create prosperity and promote the general welfare of community.

We do not expect to please every body. That is a very difficult task to perform. There was a newspaper man once who pleased every body— but that was a long time ago, and that editor— he died, and when we get to pleasing every body, we want to die too.

We want every man, woman and child in this entire neighborhood to come in early and subscribe. Our paper will do you good. No well regulated family can afford to be without it. It will drive away sorrow. It will banish pain. It will kill rats. It will cure corns. It is death on bedbugs and fleas—and only Two-and-a-half a year!

RUNNING A NEUTRAL PAPER.

One among the hardest things for a poor man to do is to publish a newspaper, that is supposed to be *Neutral in Politics*, especially in a small town, where it takes the help of every man and woman in the vicinity to keep the "machine" in running order. In such cases it is difficult for any one to maintain the spirit of true independence that should be manifested by all American citizens; yet under such circumstances, the financial condition of the poor editor too often renders it necessary for him to be decidedly accommodating with his politics.

It is a difficult task to ride fourteen horses at one time, but that is just about what the editor-in-chief of a "one-horse" paper often has to do or get "throwed." I have tried it, and I hope that all of my "victims," in the goodness of t h e i r hearts, will forgive me.

It is a little this way. A Republican candidate walks into our office, hands us five dollars and says: "Insert my card in your paper; give it a conspicuous position, and give me a rousing send-off; and after I am elected I will do the handsome thing by you." We say (after pocketing that *five*), "All right, my honored friend; after my paper comes out this week, your miserable opponent will stand *no show whatever*," and then we sit down and write him up *for all he is worth*.

A few days after this, a Democratic candidate walks in, lays his five dollars upon the altar of unadulterated patriotism and says: "Mr. Editor, I want you to insert my card; give me a g o o d square notice, and after election I expect to be able to do something for you that will enable you to remove to the County Seat and establish a daily journal." After shoving his little *five* into our faded jeans (to keep company with its brother who had gone in before), we say: "All right, all right, old friend, I will fix you up in good shape—and don't you forget it, and if you can't "get away" with that Republican in a fair race, it will be "good-bye country," and then we sit down and write him up for *more than he is worth.*

Soon after, in comes a Prohibition candidate, throws down two-and-a-half and says: "I am out for office; I want my card inserted at the head of your editorial column. We are going to make a clean sweep this fall, and for the sake of the cause, I want you to "whoop 'er up." After coaxing that *two-and-a-half* into our pocket, to become the companion of the money of the 'publican and sinner, we say: "All right, and if you will promise, after you are elected, to give the editor of this paper the job of digging up all the grape-vines in the State, you can rely upon this paper to whoop things up generally, for it claims to be a "whoopist" from Hoop-pole township."

The next caller is an Independent candidate, who says: "I want you to insert my card—top of the column—here's two dollars, I'll hand you the balance next Saturday; I shall also expect a big "blow" in your next issue." I absorbed his ducats, saying: "Correct, my valued friend,your card will be duly inserted, and as to the "blow," when my paper comes out you shall hear the voice of a *hurricane* sounding your praises and extolling your virtues. You are as good as elected now."

So goes the world. Each candidate leaves our office, confident that he has a strong ally in one paper at least; and each one leaves the editor feeling remarkably good and excessively guilty in the "five-part act" he is endeavering to perform —"all for the sake of Eliza;" and while he may not be able to materially assist all the candidates who have so generously given him a share of their patronage, he generally does the best he can to harm them as little as possible.

I will conclude this article by saying, that it is my earnest desire to see the principles of justice and right triumph, and earnestly hope that men will vôte upon every occasion, to maintain those principles which they conscientiously believe to be RIGHT—and may the Lord have mercy upon that man, who for any consideration whatever, votes contrary to his honest opinion.

MEMORIAL ADDRESS.

The following is my little address, which was read in the Ceme-
tery at Los Gatos, California, May 30th, 1884. I insert it as a slight
tribute of love and respect for the "boys who wore the blue."

COMRADES of the Grand Army of the Republic
and fellow citizens: You are all familiar with the
object that calls us together in this quiet resting
place of the dead, this pleasant Spring morning.
Almost twenty years have passed away since
the last rebel flag was lowered before the victorious armies of the Union, and the white-winged
angel of Peace found a welcome in every valley,
and on every mountain, hill and plain in this
Republic; and you have not forgotten how our
hearts thrilled with new-born rapture when the
glad news flashed from ocean to ocean, telling us
the cruel war was over and the Union preserved.
Soon after the great struggle, our noble Government set apart the 30th of May as a National
Holiday, dedicated to the memory of the fallen
heroes who died that the Nation might live; and
for the past seventeen years the beautiful custom
of strewing flowers on the graves of our dead soldiers has been annually observed with a regularity and devotion that teaches the lesson that patriotism and loyalty are yet revered and held sacred by the American people.

Three old soldiers have found here, their last
resting place in this silent village of the d e a d ,
and while we, as comrades may not have known
them personally, it is enough for us to know that
they all kept step to the music of the Union.
One followed the flag over the burning sands of
the Rio Grande, in the strife with Mexico—the
others rallied to the defense of the Union in the
last great struggle—all were loyal soldiers—and
that is enough for comrades of the Grand Army
of the Republic to know; and while the scenes of
their child-hood and the friends of their youth
may be in the far East, near where Atlantic's billows roll, we, their surviving comrades find the
grass growing on their graves under the sunny
skies of California; and our soldier hearts are stirred with those memories that stretch from the
first call to arms, to the muster in, the camp, the
weary march, the grim battle-field, the gloomy
hospital and prison pen—even to the very gates
of death—only, we trust, to find their echoes in
Heaven.

Comrades of the old crusade: the Grand Army
of the Republic will soon be no more.   The last
echo of the tread of that mighty host that once
shook the soil of this Republic from the St. Law-
rence to the Gulf, will soon be hushed, as the last
survivor glides into the shadows of the G r e a t
Beyond; yet believe me when I say, the glorious deeds achieved by the Grand Army of the
Republic will live and be honored, long after the
towering monuments of man's architectural skill,
which to-day stands firm, shall have mouldered
into oblivion.

MY FOREIGN POLICY.

THE United States of America is certainly the greatest Republic that has ever existed, and I am proud to be able to write these words; but with all its greatness and grandeur, I am inclined to think that in some respects, this Government is too magnanimous—too generous to do itself justice; and especially does this seem true in regard to the broad invitation to the inhabitants of the Old World to come here and make their homes, and do just as they please after they get here, where they are allowed to act upon the principle that "this is a free country;" and this generous invitation from "Uncle Sam" has certainly been taken advantage of by a class of people who are of no benefit to any country, and whose presence and influence (especially when the right of suffrage has been obtained), is much greater, and far more dangerous (if used in the wrong direction), in a Republic than in a Monarchy; and to remedy this evil, I would hail with delight, the passage of a law that would compel *all foreigners,* before landing upon American soil for the purpose of making their homes here, to furnish a reliable certificate for good character— and that would be no difficult task to impose upon any good citizen.

If this was done, it would have the effect to prevent Asia and Europe from sweeping their jail dust and much of their filthy slum and garbage of humanity into this country; for there is a prevailing opinion that when a man gets to be too vile and too mean to live either in Asia or in Europe, he is shipped to the United States; and he comes for what? To bid defiance to our laws, to poison society with his vile presence—to help to swell the criminal record, and often to dictate with insolent tongue as to how this Government shall be conducted.

Good citizens—be they rich or poor, should always receive a hearty welcome, but for one, I am sorry to see this great and generous Republic being made the resorvoir for the trash of *all other nations.*

WEEK DAY SERMON.

"Come and let us Reason together."

THIS COUNTRY is pretty well represented with Churches, and new religious organizations are springing into existence almost every year. In a word, there is no lack of Churches, but is genuine Christianity gaining ground? Is the World growing better? These are questions that should engage the attention of all thinking minds.

I do not claim to be a model of Christian piety, neither am I an Infidel: on the contrary, I am a firm believer in the kind of Christianity that *does* Christian work. But it is painfully true, and greatly to be regretted, that the practice of a great many professing Christians is too often at variance with their preaching and profession, and while this does not injure the true faith, it certainly has a tendency to c h e c k its progress throughout the world. (This article refers to no particular place or locality, but applicable to all).

More *work* and less *talking*, more *charity* and less *style*, is what the Church needs to-day.

Instead of getting together in little select *sets* and *circles*, and rehearsing the stereotyped phrase, such as: "What a pity it is this or that neighbor is such a wicked sinner," would it not be better, my Christian reader, if you would mix up a little with the rude and wicked elements—take a walk now and then among the wrecks of frail humanity and try what a little genuine assistance will accomplish.

When you see a man—a neighbor—"going to the bad," do not go and tell all creation about it, and then watch him from your window as he passes by, but appoint yourself "a committee of one" to go to his assistance and do your best to rescue him; and if you find that you have no influence over that man, then hunt up some o n e who has, and in nine cases out of ten, good results will follow. Do not stand aloof for fear that some of your "*set*" may discover you in bad company, for if you wish to reform depraved humanity you must go where it is. Christ was found in company with publicans and sinners, and we have no evidence to show that He was ashamed of it. If your field or garden is foul with weeds, you cannot talk the weeds out at long range.

Temperance Organizations are very good in their way, if they are blessed with a good, active *working* force, but "red tape" alone will n e v e r check the tide of Intemperance.

Faith is a good thing to have, especially if it is based upon Truth and Justice, but *faith* without *works* is dead. And the same may be said of the Christian religion. If it is practiced, it is the grand causeway that leads from Earth to Heaven; but if our religion is *all profession* and *no practice*, then it availeth nothing.

Take the civilized world over, there seems to be a perfect *deluge* in *preaching*, and a most fearful *drought* in *practice!*

As a rule, we love to see new and handsome Church edifices erected in our midst. We also love to hear the deep tones of the grand organ helping to swell the chorus of praise to God. We love to see our Church buildings fitted up with everything necessary to render them comfortable and attractive:—frescoed walls and decorated ceilings, fine carpets, elegant pews and brilliant chandeliers, and an eloquent minister who is well worth two thousand dollars a year (and who wouldn't preach Christ for a cent less), and everything else to correspond. This is all very nice and would be all right if it was in accordance to the example that Christ left for His followers; but do these continued efforts to "lay our neighbor's Church in the shade," have a tendency to please God and spread the Gospel?   That is the question, and it is a serious one. And when the unceasing Fair and Festival is held and the untiring hat goes around for the benefit of the new organ, new window-curtains, the choir, or a new carpet, or to have the pews re-painted, or for a "little more stylish" decoration, or a softer cushioned seat for the new minister, or to send another missionary to the far-away heathen—I often imagine that I can hear the plaintive voice of some poor neighbor's child asking for food and raiment; and especially when the the contribution box goes around for the benefit of the heathen in far-off lands, I feel like exclaiming: Merciful God, open the eyes, ears and hearts of this people, that they may be constrained to scatter more of their surplus cash among the ignorant, starving, naked and destitute, who can be found at all times—everywhere—all over this Gospel lighted land of ours—for "the poor we have always with us." And although he may have little else to boast of, he who hath *Charity* for his poor and needy neighbor, is *almost a Christian.*

ARMY REMINISCENCE.

(The following, I extract from my old journal of Camp Life in 1861, which I think may be read with interest by old soldiers now living, and also by the Sons of Veterans, who will soon take our places on Life's battle-field).

Headquarters 17th Regiment Ill's., Vol., Inf'y.

REGIMENTAL ORDERS.

Camp Mather, Peoria, Illinois, May 23, 1861.

ORDER No. 1.   The Commandants of Companies in which there are vacancies in the commissioned officers, will parade their respective Companies at their quarters at 10 o'clock A. M., of this date, for the purpose of holding elections to fill said vacancies.

ORDER No. 2.   Until further orders, the following programme for daily exercise will be adopted.

Officers meeting—6:30 A. M.

Officers drill—7:30 to 9:30 A. M.

Non-commissioned officers not on duty, drill at 7:30 A. M.

Company drill 9:30 to 11:30 A. M.

Company drill 2 to 4 P. M.

Dress Parade 5 P. M.

ORDER No. 4. Until further orders the Commandants of each Company will cause the side arms of all privates under their immediate control to be delivered up to a commissioned officer of each company to be held by him until actually needed; subject to such care by the owner of the same as may be necessary for their preservation in good order.

ORDER No. 5. Hereafter, no spirituous liquors shall be introduced into camp by any person or persons whatsoever, except by or under the direction of the assistant Surgeon and all sentinels upon post are hereby strictly enjoined to use great diligence in preventing the violation of the foregoing order.

ORDER No. 6. There shall be four roll calls a day as follows:

1st. Reveille will be made on the company parade by the Orderly sergeants under the supervision of a commissioned officer of the company. Upon the drums being beat the men will fall in in two ranks without regard to height, facing to the front; the music having ceased to beat, the Orderly sergeant will call the roll and report to his officer all absentees. Immediately after Reveille, the men will, under the direction of the chiefs of their squads, proceed to put their tents and quarters in order, and the Guard house by the guard or prisoners.

2nd. Breakfast call will beat at 7 A. M.

3rd. Dinner call will be beat and the roll will be called at the time prescribed in Regimental orders, the men forming as above stated.

4th. Retreat. At the first call, the men will fall in as above stated, and upon the proper order being given, will stand at rest until the music shall cease, when the roll will be called by the Orderly sergeant officer superintending.

5th. Tattoo. The roll will be called at Tattoo, also under the supervision of an officer of the Company.

ORDER No. 7. Until further orders, the different calls will be beat and the roll called as follows:

1st. Reveille. 5 o'clock, A. M.

2nd. Doctor's call—6:30, A. M.

3rd. Breakfast call—7 o'clock, A. M.

4th. Call for Guard mounting, 8:45, A. M.

5th. Drummers' call for practice, 10:30, A. M.

6th. Orderly Sergeants' call, 12, M.

7th. Drum call, 1 o'clock, P. M. (roll call).

8th. Drummers' call for practice, 2, P. M.

9th. Retreat. At Sun-set. (Roll call).

10th. Tattoo at 9 o'clock, P. M.—Taps at 9-30;

Calls for Drill and evening Parade, as well as for Fatigue, will be beat at the time specified in Regimental order No. 2.

By order, L. F. Ross, Col. Com'd'g.

LAST ORDERS OF THE 17th ILLS., V. I.,
BEFORE ITS DEPARTURE FOR "DIXIE."

Headquarters, Camp Mather, June 14th, 1861.

Regimental Order No. 10. The following order will be observed and enforced by each Company commandandant on the 16th inst:

Two days rations will be drawn and prepared by the several messes in each Company, the same to be cooked and prepared for transportation on the evening of the 16th inst.

Dress parade will take place on the 16th inst. at 5 o'clock, P. M.

Reveille will be beat at 4 A. M. on 17th inst.

Breakfast at 5 A. M. on the 17th inst.

The baggage and camp equipage will be packed ready for transportation at 7:30 A. M.

The Regiment, accompanied by music, will leave the Camp at 8:30 A. M.

Embarkation on Steamboats: Sam Gaty and LaSalle, at Peoria wharf at 9:30 A. M.

Company commandants will detail a Sergeant and file of men to be stationed under command of a commissioned officer on boats at the Company quarters, to superintend the baggage of each Company.

No arrangements for cooking other than preparing coffee will be furnished on the Boats.

The usual routine of Guard duty, under the supervision of the officer of the Day and officer of the Guard, will be strictly observed on board of the Boats.

By order of

LEONARD F. ROSS,
(Col. commanding 17th Reg. Ills., V. I.

CENTENNIAL GREETING.

(First published in Crete, Nebraska, January 1st, 1876).

To the bright and sunny South-land,
    Where the queen of beauty walks;
To the Valleys and the Mountains,
    And to the Northern Lakes,
To Pacific's Golden Gate-way,
    To the Eastern coast of Maine;
With a happy New Year's Greeting,
    We come to you again.

To greet the American people,
    Of all ages—great and small,
From the youngest in the family,
    To the father of them all.
'Tis a big page in our history,
    For the outside world to read,
Of the many grand projections
    We've achieved with lightning speed;

While Earthquakes and Revolutions
    Have sank some countries down,
This great American Nation
    Still proudly marches on;
And this whole united people—
    Ever at work or on the way,
Have carried on their business,
    And kept the World at bay!

That glad day was just dawning—
That set the hills aglow,
Proclaiming our Independence—
ONE HUNDRED YEARS AGO!
Now, our sails they whiten every sea,
With the Starry Flag unfurled;
And our Country it is honored
Throughout the entire world.

One glance at proud America—
(O, we love to write the name),
Is enough to make our school-boys
Climb up the steps of Fame;
For the road to Honor's Temple
Is nowhere so easy trod—
As it is in Free America,
Upon her sacred sod.

From the green hills of New England,
To where Pacific's breakers roar,—
From the coast of grim Alaska,
Clear down to our Southern shore—
We humbly thank our Great Creator,
That our country is at peace—
And the old American Eagle
Proudly soars o'er all the space.

Out upon the mighty ocean,
And on every foreign strand,
There is a strong impression that
Our Flag's upheld by God's own hand;
And we, as true Americans,
Should pray to Israel's God,
That no other Flag but ours shall ever
Find a foot-hold on our sod.

We are Republican to the centre,—
Always vote the Union "STRAIGHT,"
For that we think, is the safest Ticket,
To carry us through the "NARROW GATE;"

And if there are any FAVORS shown,
  Up in that World of Light,—
We believe the old "Army of the Union"
  Will be formed upon the "RIGHT."

    *   *   *   *   *

With the misty curtain rising—
  Rising up from memory's shore,
Comes the echo of familiar foot-steps,
  Rising high above the roar,—
With the bright blue sky above us—
  With our feet upon the span
That binds the ever-present
  With the Past and Future-land :—
Comes the feeling in our bosom,
  Comes the mist into our eyes,
As we watch the scenes receding,
  With the year that backward flies.

Dear readers : while cherished memories,
  Are clustering 'round us here,
Let us form new resolutions,
  For a better life, this year.
Let us all be known hereafter
  For the Good that we can do :
And scatter joy and gladness
  Wherever we may go ;
And though storms may toss and rock us
  From morning until night—
Let us fight Life's fitful battles,
  On the side of Truth and Right.

FOURTH OF JULY IN AMERICA.

(For the benefit of all who dwell Between the Tides).

FRIENDLY READER, I do not care where y o u may have lived, where you now live, or where you may live in future, but I do wish to impress up-on your mind the fact, that I consider the American Fourth of July the biggest day on top of this continent "by a large and constantly increasing majority."

Only one hundred and ten years ago, the American colonies declared their independence of Great Britain, and maintained their Independence after seven years of bloody war. Since that period, the progress of the United States has been so great and so rapid as to claim the attention and win the admiration of the entire World.

Step by step "Uncle Sam" has marched forward, carrying the Star Spangled Banner from the Eastern coast of Maine, to the white sands that strew the shores of the great Pacific, and to-day the United States of America is acknowledged as the grandest and most powerful nation on the globe—its millions of people enjoying liberties, advantages and blessings enjoyed by the inhabitants of no other country. Let us ever remember the cost of this grand structure of Liberty, and train our children to cherish with affection, and guard with zealous care the priceless boon of Freedom bestowed upon us by the forefathers of this Republic—the noble men who fought, bled and died in "the days of '76."

As I previously remarked: the Fourth of July is the biggest day on the American continent by several tons; at least such is the impression that I received when a boy—and I think so yet.

Take away all other luxuries, but give me the good old-fashioned Fourth of July once a year, with its old-time patriotic purity and enthusiastic double-geared jubil-jollification characteristics or give me—a rest. The Fourth of July is t h e birth-day of American Liberty, and do not forget to remember the circumstance.

When the glorious Fourth comes around, let the bells ring out over all this land of ours. Fling the Starry Banner to the breeze. Turn your boys loose and let them shout until they are hoarse.

Let everybody celebrate. If you cannot go to town and join the big procession, celebrate the day at home. Let the songs of patriotism go up from every valley, plain, and mountain-top from the sands of the Pacific to the blue waters of the Atlantic—from the shores of grim Alaska to the gulf of Mexico. Sing the 'Star Spangled Banner,' "Yankee Doodle," "Hail Columbia"—and hurrah for "Uncle Sam."

Let every little outside consideration rip, ravel, and get loose in the shank and run down at the heel; but when the Fourth of July comes along, don't forget to rise up "sooner in the morning."

A CHAPTER ON "MOVING."

"HALF THE WORLD IS ON WHEELS."

THE following is my experience on *moving*, and I give it for the benefit of t h o s e of my readers who are unacquainted with the "ups and downs" of those individuals who have been persistent in their efforts to find "a better country," and who, as a general rule, have found that that "some-. thing better" lay "just beyond" the goal of their ambition.

As the Reader is already aware, I first came to California in 1864 and returned in 1866; and in 1874, with my family, I came back to California, and in October of the same year, went to Clinton, Missouri, near which place I purchased a small farm; but owing to the appearance of innumerable grasshoppers, I became discouraged and in the Summer of 1875, I got the opportunity of exchanging my real estate for a printing office, which was located in Fayette, Howard county (Mo). This office had been closed on a chattel mortgage, and one of the conditions of the trade was, that I was to get possession of the office as it stood, in Fayette, and put it into operation in that town or take it away as I saw fit.

With my family I went to Fayette, got possession of the office, and then interviewed the people of the town in regard to the proper course to pursue, and I soon found that the majority were decidedly opposed to the office being removed, and promised me ample support if I would stay and not meddle too much in politics.

I found Fayette to be a wealthy town of nearly 3,000 inhabitants and the county seat of Howard county, and contained a fine University—large Tobacco manufactories, and was surrounded by a fertile country, and very thickly settled with a class of wealthy farmers, who devoted their time to raising tobacco, grain and stock. I would gladly have settled there, but the scars of the Great Civil War were so apparent upon every hand, I felt satisfied that I would be placing myself in a very embarrassing position to remain.

As this is about the last chapter in my Book, I will particularize a little. When I came to Fayette, I left my household effects at the railroad depot in Clinton, with instructions to hold them subject to my order; and to show just how an Illinoisan could scarcely realize what was the matter with him in old Missouri, I will give an illustration by telling the truth as follows: In the first place the man who had been closed out on the mortgage was a six footer, wore a long-tailed black frock coat and a plug hat, and he also appeared to regard my purchase of the office as an infringement on his rights; and to say the least, it seemed an embarrassing position for me. (For convenience sake I will call the former owner of the printing office by the familiar name of Smith (but it was not Smith by any means).

After more talk with the citizens, I concluded to revive the newspaper in Fayette; and I accordingly went to the depot and sent a dispatch to Clinton, saying: "Send my household goods on first train." Alas! how often we act in too great haste, for as I passed the building in which my material was stored, I beheld my predecessor— Smith, standing at the foot of the stairs; and it only took him about two minutes to convince me that it would be decidedly unwise for me to put his old machinery into operation. Smith was in a bad humor and I do not blame him much for being so. I began to reflect. I was a stranger in Missouri, and liable to be "taken in out of the gloaming;" and I again repaired to the depot and sent a second dispatch, reading: "Don't ship my

goods until further orders;" and then, while retracing my steps, a corner grocer hailed me and
said: "Mr., I understand that you are going to
start up Smith's old paper. I am glad of it; and
although we may not agree on politics, if you can
run a newspaper, all right, and we won't quarrel,
and by the way, if you are inclined to have the
"shakes," I've got some of the best old ague medicine in the back-room that you ever put under
your nozzle. Stranger, come in."

Reader, don't be hard on "yours truly." I was
nearly scared to death. I walked into his back-
room as weak as an infant. I came out feeling
seven times bigger than Goliath and four times
as stout as Samson; and about ten minutes after
that, I made a grand rush for the depot, and sent
out dispatch No. 3, saying "Bring on my goods,
bring 'em in a hurry and don't monkey around
in regard to incidental expenses. My family are
here and we are very anxious to get to housekeep-
ing," and then I sauntered up to town, and began to inquire for Smith. I found the gentleman
engaged in the apparently pleasant pastime of
trying to hold up the side of a tobacco warehouse
size 44 by 60 feet. I cautiously approached, and
intimated that I was a representative from Illinois, California and all way stations—and understood that he was "looking for me." I also gent-
ly reminded him of the fact that I was a distant

relative of an individual who had passed the sunny years of his childhood in "Posey county." In answer,Smith informed me that owing to his having a contract to hold up that tobacco warehouse for an hour or so, it would be extremely difficult for him to see me before morning. Acting upon the impulse of the moment, I went back to the depot, and sent another dispatch which read as follows: "Mr. Operator, don't s e n d anything. Don't do anything.   Don't let anything whatever pass over your road until you hear from me."

Upon returning to the central part of town, I met one of the influential citizens of the place, and he advised me to remain in Fayette, promising me his assistance. My next move was to the depot, where I sent another dispatch which read about as follows: "Agent at Clinton, send my stuff right along. Send everything you can get your hands on. Send everybody here who wishes to settle in a live town, for things will be booming here inside of ten days—and after you send everything else—*send your bill.*" (You see that I was getting a little excited). Once more I went up on the busy streets, and soon met another influential citizen, and he said: "I understand that you think of reviving Smith's old paper. We would be glad to have you remain, but I would not advise you to dip into politics too deep on the start, as some of our people still feel a little sore over the old issues. Once more I began to reflect on the peculiarity of my situation; and this time I fully made up my mind to take the office out of Fayette. It was then early in the morning, and I walked rapidly up the street. At the foot of the stairway leading to my office was Smith, and he was in a passable good humor. I approached him and said: "Friend Smith, the printing outfit upstairs is mine. I bought it in good faith. Let us be candid with each other. Let us be friends. We have no quarrel. Let us talk *business*. It would be an annoyance to you if I started up your old paper in this town. It would also annoy your friends; and to show you that I am disposed to act right about this matter, I propose to take the office out of Fayette. Help me do this, and I will ship it to Clinton."

This touched the man's better nature, and he promised to lend a helping hand and oversee the packing up of the material. We shook hands, and I gave Smith the key and put him to work and I once more went to the depot and sent another dispatch to Clinton which read about as follows: "Gentlemen: Drop everything. Don't touch a bedstead, cook-stove, rocking-chair, door mat or wood-box that belongs to me or any other man until you see me, and after you see me, *don't do anything.*"

I then went out on the street and hired fourteen of the most powerful negroes to be found,

and put them to work under the supervision of
friend Smith, who worked hard and faithfully to
get everything packed up in good shape; I also
hired one wagon and two drays to convey the
material to the depot, and by four o'clock in the
afternoon, my entire establishment, and my family, were on board the cars; but just before our
train started, a freight train came dashing in and
the agent came up and tapped me on the shoulder and said: "A lot of household goods has just
arrived to your address; what shall be done with
them?" I said: "That's all right. That's perfectly right—it's more than right, and it serves me
just right. Ship those goods back to Clinton, unless you get a countermanding order by telegraph
before I get there." As it happened, we arrived
in Clinton without any further mishap—and only out of pocket the paltry sum of *one hundred
and fifteen dollars*, for railroad fare and freight,
hotel bills, telegraphing, draying, manager and
negro help—*cheap enough!*

At Clinton I established the *"Henry County
News,"* ran it for six weeks, and no doubt would
have added largely to the population of that county, by drawing upon Illinois for recruits, but just
about that time, I received a very encouraging
letter from a relative in Crete, Nebraska, telling
me that Crete was situated in the geographical
centre of the United States, and that it was more

than highly probable that the Capitol of the U. S., would be located in Crete—or somewhere else, (I am now inclined to think it will be located at some other point), and if I wanted to "strike while the iron is hot," to come to Crete without delay."

This sounded like business, and I closed out my paper in Clinton, packed my material, hired a whole car at a cost of one hundred and sixty dollars, and "lit out" for Crete at a pace t h a t would have put "Maud S" in the shade by several lengths.

This was in November, 1875, and the weather was getting decidedly *chilly* in that latitude.

When we arrived in Crete we found that the principal part of the town was located—"on the map," consequently, houses were scarce and rents very high; but I finally secured a building that was all hall below and several rooms, separated by thin board partitions, above. I piled the office material on the first floor and piled my family into the cheerless, wind-swept rooms above, and in this domicil we battled with the elements for several weeks, when more comfortable quarters were procured; and now, as I write this article, I look back with a shudder, and wonder how we managed to survive. Winter came with cold, sweeping winds and blinding snow storms; and night after night I was compelled to keep a big stove red-hot, putting in the long dreary hours, dozing on a rude bench—only to be aroused at intervals by the chilly warning that it was time to pour in more coal.

I hired a printer from Hastings, but after five weeks, his father wrote for him to come to help his younger brother to follow a rope that reached from the house to the barn, to aid them in finding their way to feed the horses and cattle! I told him to go. Then I hired a printer from Omaha, but he soon had his ears frozen while he was engaged in deciphering my manuscript, in front of the type racks, and he returned to h i s home on the banks of the "Big Muddy," for surgical treatment. Then I hired a Bohemian printer (at that time nearly half the population of Crete were Bohemians), and with the aid of my Bohemian compositor, by carrying a hot brick in each coat pocket and wearing fur-lined buckskin gloves, we managed to get out several issues of the paper during the winter; but when they did come out they looked as if they had b e e n blasted by lightning and then fired from a siege gun charged with cold ink. That winter my office stove consumed a car-load of coal and more than 150 bushels of corn—and with all this outlay, we seldom got the office thoroughly warmed up until Spring came, but then it was too late to soothe my damaged temper. The other paper in Crete was run by a couple of good, clever men and it was mutually understood by all of us that it would be folly for both of our institutions to attempt to winter a second time in Crete, unless a coal-mine should be discovered in close proximity, or unless more land be planted to corn. and finally they proposed to purchase my subscription list and all my surplus material, and I accepted the offer, and the next week I published my *Valedictory*, of which, the following is an extract:

"When this paper goes out, the days of the *Crete Sentinel* will be numbered.

What brought us here, or why we came, matters little—suffice to say, we are aware of the fact that *we are here now!* We expected to find Crete large enough and financially able to support two newspapers, and we were just egotistical enough to think that it would take the quint-essence of "Starvation Corner" to prevent our making, at least, a living, (and it did).

It is unnecessary to enter into details, as to how we planned, worked, tugged, lived and dressed; and how we went from coal to corn, and from corn to corn-*cobs*—and still drifted shoreward— And the *bills*, how they kept *coming in*, and our money kept *going out*. Coal bills, corn bills, cob bills, rent bills, paper bills, ink bills, store bills, express and freight bills, following each other in such rapid succession that we almost expected to see the original old "Nebraska Bill" put in an appearance.

After drawing two hundred dollars from an Illinois deposit and the proceeds of forty acres of Missouri land, and sinking it all "for the benefit of Crete," we find ourself on the *ragged edge*, and now, as the conversation around our dining table has simmered down to simply: "pass the *salt* and help yourself to the *mustard*," we think it full time to suspend further operations in the valley of the *Blue*. Peerless valley, and most fitly named; an indigo shower could not deepen your financially depressed borders at this time.

It may seem humiliating for the publisher of a newspaper to be compelled to suspend, through a lack of support from its patrons, or from lack of ability on the part of the publisher; but we say in all sincerity, that no mortal man ever stepped from the tripod of a village newspaper office with feelings of more heart-felt happiness at the prospects of an early departure from the field of his recent labors, than we do to-day. Many a better man than the writer, and with far brighter hopes and prospects for a brilliant future than ever flitted through his brain, has been forced to yield to the adversities and perplexities that so often figure in the great drama of Life.

We go from your midst, encouraged with the thought that we did the best we could, and we leave Saline county, we hope, in no worse condition financially, than it was when we first landed upon its virgin soil; and it is our earnest hope that the lowering clouds of your financial depression will soon be wafted from these plains by the healing breezes of returning prosperity, and in the *after while*, when our work is done, we hope to meet you (Bohemians and all) in *a better country than Nebraska*, where grasshoppers are never seen, and where the voice of the hurricane is never heard—where droughts and floods never come, and where Nebraska farmers won't be bothered with lightning-rod peddlars, and where business men who never advertise are unknown. There is where I hope to meet you. And while your pilgrimage is extended in this *Vale of affliction*, may your flocks and your herds increase, and may your good deeds increase more than all else, and while we hope that our feet will soon press the soil of another land, although we may look back and shudder at the recollections of the cold winters of Nebraska, we shall ever cherish a kindly feeling for the many warm friends we found in Crete."

The year of 1876 was probably one of the hardest years experienced by Nebraska farmers.

From Crete I removed to Lincoln, the Capital of Nebraska, where I opened a Job Printing office, but soon found that I had struck that city in the wrong time, for the grasshoppers were already beginning their march of destruction—going through the State, leaving devastated fields and desolation behind. Business of all kinds was depressed and property of every description was to be had "almost for the asking." Within three blocks of the business centre, and of the Capitol building, at that time, I was offered nice homes at prices ranging from five hundred to one thousand dollars! Everybody was discouraged; all the main roads leading from all parts of Nebraska to the Missouri river, were crowded with the covered wagons of the settlers of Nebraska, going East —*fleeing from their homes!* Then was the time I should have remained. But everybody else wanted to get out of Nebraska, and I concluded that I wanted to go too—and I went. "Went where?" (I imagine I hear the reader asking). Why, back to California, of course! I sold my presses, packed up the balance of my printing material, loaded everything on board the cars (including my family), and one pleasant evening in September, 1876, found us in Omaha, ready to try the realities of Life once more in the Far West.

This time I had an idea that I would like San Diego, but while in San Francisco I did not find

a man that had been to San Diego, who expressed a desire to return; but as I wished to look at
least, at a portion of Southern California, we took
a Steamer for Ventura, the county seat of Ventura county, about 450 miles South of San Francisco, leaving orders with the agent of the C. P. R.
R., to ship my goods to Ventura upon their arrival from the East, as I had no idea of returning.

We arrived at Ventura in due season, found it
to be a very nice little town, but unfortunately
(as I then thought), a second newspaper had recently been established, and consequently there
was no field for me in that direction, and I have
since been glad that such was the case. I also
found at that time (I do not know how it is now)
that house rents were too high for common sense
reasoning; building material of all kinds was also very high and stove-wood was selling at from
ten to twelve dollars per cord. The little valley
in which Ventura is situated seemed to be of a
very fertile character, but to the writer, coming
from the broad prairies of Nebraska, there did
not seem to be enough tillable land in the whole
valley to make more than two or three ordinary
sized farms; but I have been told that Ventura
county is well adapted to stock-raising—also producing large quantities of honey and coal oil—
but of course I can't help that.

We remained in Ventura about ten days, and learning, from apparently reliable sources, that lumber, rents and fuel "got higher" the farther South one went, I made up my mind to take the "back track," and accordingly I wrote a letter to the freight agent in San Francisco, telling him to hold my goods until further orders, and then I wrote a letter to my brother in Illinois, telling him that we had arrived safely, and all were well. By a strange freak of luck, I put the letter for my brother in the envelope addressed to the freight agent, and *vice versa*, and sent them off! My brother received his letter some ten days afterwards, but apparently did not clearly understand what business he had with a San Francisco freight office. The agent also received his letter, and supposing from its contents that "everything w a s lovely," sent my entire outfit down to Ventura by the first Steamer. (For one time at least, the Railroad Company acted with an alacrity that was truly surprising), and that little mistake of mine cost me nearly one hundred dollars. Again I solemnly aver that, "such is Life." But I must hurry up. We returned to San Francisco, went from there to Petaluma and opened a Job Printing office, but at that time the diphtheria was raging there in an epidemic form. I remained only about four weeks, and then went to Cloverdale, at which place I established a newspaper, and actually remained there until the following Spring, 1877, when I again sold out and with my family went back to Lincoln, Nebraska! Here I remained until the following Spring, 1878, when I traded another farm for a printing outfit and moved it to Seward, the county seat of Seward county, (Neb). At this place I continued in the newspaper busines until some time in June, 1879, when I sold out to Mr. Jas. H. Betzer, who changed the name of the paper from the Seward county *Advocate* to that of the Blue Valley *Blade.* My successor, Mr. Betzer, besides being a perfect gentleman in every respect, proved to be a most excellent newspaper man, and at this writing, the *Blade* under his excellent management, still waves, and is recognized as one of the best local papers published in Nebraska.

In september, 1879, with my family, I again r e t u r n e d to California, and soon after my arrival on the Pacific coast, I went up to Cloverdale and purchased my old "paper mill," and ran it until the next Summer, 1880, when I a g a i n sold out and went back to—where? Why to Lincoln, Nebraska, as a matter of course. (It looks as if we are making this track rather hot).

This move (so we all said) was to be *our last move*; (and it did come very near letting us out) but the winter of 1880–'81 was one of the severest on record. It seemed as if the very elements were fixed for our arrival.

That winter, I commenced to keep a record of the separate snow-storms of the season, but after I counted up to 67, I got angry, scratched out my journal entries and said: "Just let 'er snow."

It commenced getting *cool* in September, and in October it got to be decidedly *cold*, and kept increasing speed in the direction of the N o r t h pole, until sometime in February, 1881, it got so *intensely cold* that it was extremely dangerous for a "well disposed" man to say, "good morning" to his next door neighbor, for fear he would think he was trying to *freeze him out.* I think during that winter, from November first, 1880 to February 15th, 1881, the mercury indicated an average temperature of 20 degrees below *"Cairo!"* It was not an uncommon occurrence during that winter for passenger trains to get "stuck" in the snow-drifts and be compelled to remain all night within two miles of the city of Lincoln—a city at that time of twenty thousand inhabitants and five Railroads! I stood it all very well (for I had *come to stay*) until one morning, when I arose at an early hour (in order to keep from freezing in my little bed), but alas! during the night a heavy sleet had fallen, and the ground was covered with ice of an exceedingly *slick quality.* Our dwelling occupied a high piece of ground, sloping abruptly to the West. I opened the West door and stepped out to "view the landscape o'er,"when suddenly, my feet made a wild kick at something or other overhead, although I cannot tell to this day what I was aiming at; my head struck the edge of the porch floor, breaking off about forty cents worth of pine lumber, and then I commenced "going down hill" on a little coasting expedition of my own getting up, and never stopped until I had forced myself about half-way through an Osage orange hedge fence at the foot of the slope. I was not very badly hurt? Oh no! I was able to go right to work—that is, I was able to go right to work in about two months after this sad calamity, and then *I went to work packing up for California!* I had enough of Nebraska for the time being. (Reader, do not let this little circumstance worry you).

I think it was about the 10th of April, 1881, when I packed up for my last move to California; and among other things, I shipped a large outfit of printing material, which, together with the principal portion of my household goods and effects, reached the Union Pacific Freight Depot at Ogden, Utah, in time to be consumed in the big fire that occurred there about the 6th of May, whereby the depot, freight buildings with their contents, together with about forty loaded cars and much other valuable property was entirely destroyed. But I knew nothing of this calamity in which I was deeply interested, until several weeks afterwards, and in blissful ignorance, I roved over a large portion of California seeking for a location in which to establish a newspaper when my expected material should arrive. In justice to the Union Pacific Railroad Company, I am pleased to say, the Company paid me a fair equivalent for the loss I sustained by the fire.

This last (so far) trip proved an unlucky one for me. Heretofore in all my journeys with my family, to and from California, I had been very fortunate in getting my children through without having to pay any fare for them, but this time the fates were evidently against me, for at Omaha, when I went to the office to procure tickets for the journey, the size of my children, w h o were standing uncomfortably near, gave my case away, and I was "persuaded" to invest in *four* tickets instead of *two*! But of course, this is all between you and me, and I was not particularly caring for expenses, for I was "*going to California to stay.*"

After reaching San Francisco, I spent several weeks looking for a suitable place to locate, visiting Sacramento, Vallejo, Dixon, Auburn, Vacaville, Nevada City and several other places, but finding these fields fully occupied, I returned to San Francisco, where I had left my family, and then I commenced a vigorous search through all the Directories I could find, and then I fell back on the real estate offices—and that is just what saved me. I was referred to the "flourishing town of Saratoga," in Santa Clara county, where, my informant said, there was no newspaper, but he said there ought to be one, and if I concluded to go, he felt satisfied that I would do well.

I returned to the hotel and told my wife that our wanderings were nearly over, for I had discovered a veritable "bonanza," and that bonanza lay hidden in the village of Saratoga!

Filled with an enthusiasm that knew no bounds I boarded a train on the Southern Pacific Railroad and was soon flying in the direction of the town that needed a newspaper, and in less than three hours I stopped off at a little station called Los Gatos, and was informed that I was then within about three miles of the town of Saratoga. It was then nearly noon, and besides being very hungry, I was just about half "doubled up" with a severe attack of cramp colic. By the way, Reader, were you ever afflicted with the colic? If not, it is not your sympathy I am seeking. I first went to a hotel (the Coleman House), situated at the East end of the main (and the only) street, got my dinner, and then I told the proprietor that I wished to go to Saratoga, as I thought of establishing a newspaper at that place.

The proprietor, Mr. Coleman, told me that of the two places, he should prefer Los Gatos, as Saratoga was only a small, quiet village'with no railroad.

"Why," said he, "a Mr. Kelly is stopping here, and he can tell you all about Saratoga; he was over there yesterday, and I will call him in, if you would care to consult him." I told him to bring in Mr. Kelly. This gentleman soon came into the bar-room, when the following conversation [almost *verbatim*] ensued. I said: "Have you been in Saratogo, and if so, what do you think of the town? Mr. Kelley said: "Yes, I have been there, came from there yesterday; I was all over the place and was retracing my steps to the livery stable, when a small but viciously inclined dog ran up behind me and commenced snapping at my heels. A boy came out of a house and began calling the animal off; but I said, let him alone, for I want to carry the news back to my home that I *did* find *one* object in Saratoga that *had some life in it*,"

Kelley's narrative done the business. Saratoga lost a paper and Los Gatos gained one, as I soon established the Los Gatos Weekly *News*, which I conducted until March, 1885, when I sold the establishment to Messrs. Trantham, Webster and Suydam, it being under their excellent management at this writing.

During the past five years, Los Gatos has increased wonderfully in population, wealth, and industries, and is recognized as a place of considerable importance; and I take pleasure in saying, that the once sleepy old town of Saratoga has awakened from her slumbers, and has fallen in with the march of progression, with prospects of a Railroad to be completed the present year.

This ends my chapter on *moving* so far as the writer is concerned, and it is not likely that we will figure in as many moves in the future as in the past, for it is indeed a risky business, and I now feel more fully contented than ever before, to remain—AT HOME—for, "Our days are gliding swiftly by."

CONCLUSION.

As a great many invalids make their way to California with the hope of regaining h e a l t h , it is very natural that they should feel an anxiety as to what portion of the State would be the most suitable to their ailments.

This is a very delicate subject, and a very difficult one to treat in a fair, honest, impartial and satisfactory manner.

Thus far in my little work, I have endeavored to keep its pages free from everything that might be looked upon as an *advertisement* for any particular locality; but for the benefit of the afflicted I will say that, for people suffering from throat and lung diseases, there is a great difference of opinion, or at least a great difference in the expression of opinions. San Diego, Los Angeles, Santa Barbara, Ventura, San Luis Obispo, Monterey, Los Gatos, Saratoga, San Jose, Cloverdale, Auburn, and almost anywhere in the foot-hills of the Sierra Nevadas, and also on the slopes of the Santa Cruz mountains, are all highly recommended; but all who come and settle, even in these

highly favored and highly recommended localities, do not receive any permanent benefit—on
the contrary, many invalids who come to this
coast, come, only to find a *grave* upon its sunny
slopes—for "such is Life."

I think any new country or new location, filled with strangers, is a bad place for an invalid
in the last stage of Consumption, for after the
novelty of the change of location wears off, a
large per cent of this class speedily fret themselves into their graves, and generally die regret-
ting their removal from their old homes, old
friends and old associations.   It is my honest o-
pinion, if one can afford it, that frequent change
of location is the best medicine for the invalid
who is not too sick to travel.   Try one location
just so long as you feel that you are being benefited, and when this fails, seek the next best
place.   A change from the Eastern States to California often builds up failing health, and a great
many cases have also come under my personal
observation where people suffering from ill health
have went from California to the States East of
the Rocky mountains and were greatly benefited
by the change.   Those persons with health as the
principal object in view, should study the alti-
tude, temperature and atmosphere most suited
to their cases, and this can only be done by travel and experience.   Acting upon this principal,

more than from a real desire to be constantly *moving from place to place*, the writer has battled with chronic ailments for many long years, and I am inclined to think that the climate of Los Gatos has treated me *as well* as that of any other place that *I* have *tried*; but I honestly b e l i e v e that the State of Nebraska possesses a climate as healthy as California, but the rigorous winters of Nebraska is the great obstacle to encounter; (all people *too sick to travel, should stay at home*) but the opportunities for a man with small capital, for making an independent living are largely in favor of Nebraska. It may seem strange for a *Californian* to make this statement, but it is the *Truth in a nut-shell*.

At the present time, at least, California is *not a paradise for the poor man*, especially if he comes with the expectation of securing a home of his own, from which he can glean a living. A man with a capital of one thousand dollars, can secure a small farm in Nebraska, Kansas, or Missouri and surround himself with the comforts of life, lay up money and be independent as a king, but as a rule, he cannot do this in California—unless he comes prepared to live mostly on *climate*.

I send this Book out into the World, not expecting that it will be free from errors—on the contrary, I expect that many of its readers will differ with me in regard to many things contained therein; but that is a right that belongs to each and every individual, and as *my* opinions in regard to some things are to be found in this volume, I will leave it for others to express *their* opinions when, where and as they see fit; and if in any line I have mentioned places or persons in order to fill up the "waste places" in my manuscript, indulging in a feeble attempt at pleasantry, that may seem as having been written in an unfriendly spirit, I hope to be forgiven, for no injury or slight has been intended; and in the future days, I would be only too happy to grasp the hand of every reader of these pages, and receive from each and every one the encouraging words that recognize me as *a friend of humanity*.

What I have written in relation to California, at least so far as regards the interests of the masses who seek a home within her borders, I have written with a desire to create no false impression, so that if any are induced to come here from anything I may have written in this book, they come on their own responsibility, and after coming, will, I trust, be willing to admit that I have promised no realization of "big expectations," for the days when gold could be obtained almost for the trouble of merely picking it up, have passed away, and will never again return as they were in the good old days of yore; and the new Eldorado will have to be sought in other fields.

But there is another encouraging sign of future prosperity for California, and that is: the large tracts of land, so often to be found ten, years ago, stretching for miles, under the ownership of one individual, and used only for grazing purposes, are now being cut up, sub-divided and sold off in small tracts of ten, fifteen and twenty acres, suitable as homes for people possessed with moderate means; and many tracts, formerly supposed to be worthless for anything except pasturage, are now covered with comfortable homes, surrounded with orchards and vineyards; and in this respect, for the PEOPLE, California is a better country than it was in what has been termed its "palmy days;" and as a natural consequence, in this respect, it is growing better "as the days go by;" and when its people learn the lessons of economy, and practice them, as do our neighbors in the far East, California will develop into one of the most charming home States in this great Union.

It is difficult to wean people from extravagant habits, and a great many "old Californians" seem yet too young to realize the true worth of a dollar, and in parting with a *"twenty,"* they do not *squeeze* it half so hard as some of our E a s t e r n neighbors squeeze a *nickel*! But do not understand me to say that *all* our California brethren are proverbially given to extravagance in their expenditures—nor that *all* of our Eastern brothers are given to the habit of *pinching off the date* in parting with a nickel, but mention it merely as an illustration in comparison, and, as in either case, if the truth warranted the statement, no unpardonable sin would be committed, and no very great harm would result; but whether it be owing to climatic influence or from some other cause, I know not, but I am led to believe, as a general rule, that people grow more generous in their disposition and practice as they travel *West*; and this last sentence gives me a new idea, *i. e.* The fact that I have traveled West so often, accounts in a measure for my being *a little too generous* in many respects!

I love the Western Coast. If I did not I should not have tried so often and so persistently to wean myself from the old home of my childhood, with all its tender recollections and cherished associations.

I love the Pacific Coast, with its lovely valleys, lofty mountain ranges, clear streams of pure cold water, majestic forests, grassy slopes and blooming orchards—its sunny skies and liberal-hearted people, and would never weary listening to the swell and roar of the grand old o c e a n , whose crystal waters break upon its shell strewn shore.

But while I may be in love with California, and grow enthusiastic over its charms and attractions, I do not wish to unsettle the mind of any individual to such an extent as to cause that individual no matter where he now lives, to change his home and a living for the chances of finding something better on the strength of anything I say or may have said in relation to what suits *me*. Owing to having been engaged in the newspaper business for many years, it has been a part of "my regular business" to endeavor to induce *"all creation"* to *"come to the only live town in America,"* (at which place I was then stopping), but my newspaper days I think, are well nigh over, and although I am told that "the road to hell is paved with good resolutions," I have formed one resolution that I am determined will remain inviolate so long as I inhabit this "vale of affliction," and that is: I will never knowingly use my influence to induce any one—be he native or foreign born, to sell his home where he is making a respectable living, and change his location with the expectation of bettering his condition, unless the object be solely to regain health, and

"Tho' storms may toss and rock, and tides may swing me in their ebb and flow, from this I will not be changed."

We are all liable to make mistakes; and mistakes are much easier made than corrected. If we are so fortunate as to possess a comfortable home in Republican America with all the conveniences that the word *home* implies, it is about as much as we have a right to expect in this world; and above all other considerations, let us bear in mind the unalterable fact that, "This earth is not our abiding place. There is a realm beyond the skies, where the rain-bow never fades; where the stars are spread out before us like the beautiful islands that slumber on the bosom of the mighty ocean, to stay in our presence forever."

And it will also be well to bear in mind that riches in *gold and silver* alone, is not all that is necessary to render us happy in this life, neither is the accumulation of much wealth in gold and silver either necessary or required, to fit us for *that better life, beyond the tides*; and in our struggles after the riches of e a r t h , let us remember that, while the rich may occupy a higher station here—*there are no reserved seats in Heaven.* Only *one price* is charged for admission through the gate that opens into the New Jerusalem; and that admi sion fee is endorsed by *Faith, Hope* a n d *Charity;* "but the greatest of these is *Charity.*"

There are none so poor as to be unable to become the possessor of a ticket that guarantees a "free and unobstructed right of way" over the bridge that spans the "river Jordan"—reaching from Earth to Heaven.

I will soon close, and submit the result of my recent labors to the public, and hope to be able to recognize all the criticisms alluding to my errors (and I know there are many), with a christian fortitude at the least, equal to any emotion of pleasure that I might experience from any expression uttered in my favor.

Reader, in perusing the pages of this Book, you have been my companion. You have followed me in my wanderings from beyond the Mississippi to the sands of the Pacific; but our sojourn together as companions is well nigh over, and now, with one hand as it may seem, resting upon the ruins of the PAST, and with the other, endeavoring to push aside the big gate that opens into the hope-bordered fields of To-MORROW, I leave my parting injunction to you, and to my family, to whom this Book is dedicated:—Do not do as I may have done, but follow my *advice*, and be sober and temperate in all things. Be contented, and in future, do even as I hope to do, for I yet hope to be able to say:

> "I live for those who love me,
>   For those who know me true;
> For the heaven that smiles above me,
>   And awaits my spirit, too;
> For the Cause that lacks Assistance,
>   For the Wrongs that need Resistance,
> For the Future in the distance—
>   And the Good that I can do."

Let us be honest, faithful and earnest in o u r endeavors, and strive to do as *little evil*, and as *much good* as we can, as we drift "Between t h e Tides"—for,

> "Lives of good men all remind us,
>   We can make OUR lives sublime,
> And departing, leave behind us,
>   Foot-prints on the sands of Time."

FRIENDLY READER: Good-bye—Farewell, and may God bless you.

F*I*N*I*S.